MW01027651

to be
to is
to was

stephen c. bird

DEDICATED TO

My Friends, My Family, My Colleagues,
My Associates, My Supporters,
My Detractors, My Idols, My Mentors,
Maya Hiyuh Powuh and The Universe.

TABLE OF CONTENTS

FATHER AND SON
CROSS THE BRIDGE

It was a late afternoon in August 1970. A father was driving and his ten-year old son sat next to him in the front seat. They were riding in a beige 1970 Buick sedan, on the main north-south road that cut through the center of the village. They passed by the Amourrican Lesion as they drove southwards towards a bridge that crossed a river. While they were crossing the bridge, the son was thrown from the front seat side window, over the railing of the bridge and into the stream. The current was moving very slowly in the summer heat. The son sank to the bottom of the river. He could see clearly as he rested on the riverbed. He had his knees up to his chest and his arms folded around his knees. Strangely enough, the son was comfortable resting on the bottom of the stream. He even closed his eyes for a moment. Frankly, it was a relief. He quickly realized that he could breathe underwater. He wasn't a suicide, as far as he knew, unless he had died and was now in the afterlife, or in whatever kind of life happens after death. He wasn't a fetus, since he was now ten years old, but he felt like he'd returned to the womb. Had he been reborn? Before he'd been hurled out of the car and into the river, he'd been very sad. So sad that he'd wanted to die. But now he felt free. He became aware of a clarity and serenity that up until that time he'd never known. Being thrown out of that car and into the stream was the best thing that had ever happened to him. He had no idea what was going to transpire next. Would he stay in the water? Come out of the river and continue his human life? Evolve into a new species of amphibian? In that moment, he didn't care; he was flooded with optimism and no matter what ended up taking place, everything was going to be all right ..... His father hadn't even noticed that his son had flown out of the car window. He made a right turn onto a road immediately after crossing the bridge, and a minute later, made a right turn onto the street where he and the rest of his family lived. Thirty seconds later, he made a right turn into his driveway and then pulled into the garage of his conventional, suburban home: a two-story 1960 Colonial. Once inside the house, the father proceeded from the kitchen to his favorite armchair in the living room. He then sat down to read the evening paper ..... Outside it was hot and humid and the freshly cut grass was vivid green. Purple-black clouds were rolling in and darkening the skies. There was a lamp next to the armchair and the father turned it on. It looked like they were in for one hell of a thunderstorm.

SUNNIE DEELITE
COMES OF AGE

It was June, 1978 and Sunnie Deelite had just graduated from Mrs. Scheissbook's School for Fascist Piggies, in the Northeastern Zone of Amourrica Profunda. After the commencement ceremony, he peeled out of the school's circular, pebble-covered driveway in a rusted-out Volkswagen van and embarked on a cross-country drive to Palm Things in the Western Desert Region. He knew that he was attracted to men; he was gay, queer, a queen, a nelly, a pansy, a screamer and dying to get out of the closet. He didn't know yet whether he was a top or a bottom. Of course, he knew it was wrong to use those types of pejorative monikers to describe homosexual males. But both his politically incorrect sense of fantasy and his penchant for the taboo inspired this transgression. Sunnie had faggots on the brain, and not the white picket fence kind either. He was afraid yet fascinated by what little he knew and he was ready for adventure ….. In the late 1970's, terms such as *homonormative* and *heteronormative* were not widely used by the LGBTQ population. Gay neighborhoods were still integrated into the red-light districts of cities worldwide; back in the day, gay men were considered to be sexual outlaws who lived their lives travelling between their various urban ghettos and underworlds ….. It was June, 1978 and after arriving in Palm Things, Sunnie somehow worked up the nerve to go to one of the local pickup bars where two gay leathermen, both of them being chicken hawks, espied Sunnie the twinkie and reveled in his youthful androgyny. In both their approach and attitude, they resembled a couple of fawning, Shakespearian court jesters. Yet surprisingly, for two men who professed to live their lives as pigs, they maintained a respectful distance with Sunnie. They ascertained that he was inexperienced and would most likely be hesitant to engage in spontaneous, erotic adventures. They realized that he was not naturally precocious and that he would have to be drawn out of his shell. They went by the names of Toby and Mordred and were both older than Sunnie by about ten years. They perused him for a few minutes before introducing themselves. They then started to advise him:

Toby: We'll teach you about the real world by putting you through a trial by fire. What did you learn in Mrs. Scheissbook's School for Fascist Piggies, anyways? (*batting his eyes*) Were you attentive in class or were you distracted by your fantasies? Did you develop special friendships with any of the boys? Or were you merely one of those boring, humdrum types; the kind who are fixated solely on getting good grades, to the exclusion of the natural expression of their sexuality?

Sunnie becomes visibly uncomfortable and remains silent.

Mordred: (*breaking the silence*) It's a shame that you never attended the Szczmawgwhorets Ackademie of Sorcerie. There's so much that a young man like yourself, bursting with talent and potential, could have learned in those Not-So-Hallowed Halls!

Sunnie: (*suddenly enthused*) Yes! I did have such a longing to attend Szczmawgwhorets! But alas, mother and father forbade me to engage in the study of sorcerie. Oh, to have known, and cavorted with, the likes of Frivolous Snide and Antithesis Reticence! And how could we forget the legendary Unholie Trynytie of Higher Parterre, Traan Mrs. Beasley and Whoremoania Gangster! Oh, to have studied Herbologie and to have been trained in the upkeep of the Madrigauloise!

Toby and Mordred: (*speaking simultaneously*) YES! WHO COULD EVER FORGET THE MADRIGAULOISE! HALF CASTRATO – HALF GINSENG ROOT!

Toby: (*glistening*) And what exactly is it about Herbologie that intrigues you, Sunnie? Perchance you'd feel most at home in a greenhouse full of carnivorous plants? And when I say this, I can't help but think of Katharine Hepburn, in the role of Violet Venable, in *Suddenly Last Summer*! Why it's a must see for unformed, would-be paramours such as yourself! You can learn a lot about being in the life by watching classic Amourrica Profoundan films like that one, Sunnie! (*in a serious tone*) We can guide you; we can offer you many options. But only if you feel that you're ready.

Mordred: Don't be afraid of your girly man side, Sunnie. Or your girly girl side either, for that matter! There's so many ways to glitter and be gay. You can be a macho dominator, an outrageously effeminate over–the-top diva or even a shy, retiring wallflower!

Toby: You can be a hyper-masculine Tom of Finland bad boy or Laura Wingfield in *The Glass Menagerie*! You can fuck with people's preconceptions in this way by playing with these stereotypes! Always keep them guessing, Sunnie! And once you've perfected this special skill, no one will ever take advantage of you!

Mordred: And should you want to act, dress and be like a woman, this will have no bearing on your masculinity! In fact, being in touch with your feminine side shows that you're secure in your maleness. Get to know the woman within you, Sunnie! You'll be so glad that you did!

Sunnie: (*his hands clasped together in fervent anticipation*) Oh could I? Could I be a totally womanly man-woman? Is there anything that one can't aspire to be nowadays, as you suggest? It would be like a dream come true! Or even a nightmare, but a good kind of expressionist nightmare like *The Cabinet of Doctor Caligari*! Or perhaps a dream and a nightmare combined that's yin yang, day and night, black and white, dark and light, sun and moon.

Mordred: Say goodbye to the organic innocence of whispering Woodstock wind chimes and the Laurel Canyon dream catchers that nurtured your imagination as a child! Leave behind the yellow, green, pink and purple tie-dyed T-shirts fancied by followers of The Grateful Dead! And say hello to whatever kind of man-woman, or woman-man, you want to be! You don't have to change your sex; there are many other ways to release yourself from the limitations of your masculinity!

Toby: We'll shatter all of your illusions and create a whole set of new ones, that will be much more suited to your upcoming life-adaptation. And it's good to remember that you'll always have the pragmatic option of wearing your macho mask, especially when your survival is at stake. With that in mind, we'll buy you a rubber wardrobe, we'll take you to Boyropa for your indoctrination and we'll teach you all about sadomasochism, bondage and deprivation.

Mordred: We'll show you the ropes, literally and figuratively. We'll teach you all about role playing and school you in how to be charming and provocative at the same time.

Toby: Practice your smile in the mirror, Sunnie. Practice makes perfect!

Sunnie is overwhelmed by everything that he's hearing but is determined to make his thoughts known.

Sunnie: Well, as long as I find love, it doesn't matter what I end up being! But here's one thing that I want and that's this: good old-fashioned, mid-twentieth century, Boyropan-style fun like they had in *La Dolce Vita* and *Giulietta degli spiriti*. LOVE, LOVE, LOVE!

Toby: (*giving Mordred a knowing look*) In Palm Things, post-puritanical mores are celebrated without reservation. And the hot, dry climate of Palm Things will help you to come out of your shell and open you up.

Mordred: (*interrupting*) PALM THINGS IS ON FIRE, BABY! OH MY GODDESS IT'S ON FIRE, MISS THING!

Toby glares impatiently at Mordred.

Toby: Regarding your relocation, Sunnie: If Palm Things ends up not being your cup of tea, then how about Santa Barbital? It could function as a zone of neutrality as opposed to being showbizzy, Byzantine and Machiavellian like Lost Angelist. Are you by any chance intrigued by the divine, disco decadence of hippie lefty Scam Francisco?

Mordred: Grrrl, if you've got the chutzpah, panache and bravado to claw your way to the top, then Lost Angelist is the place to be. Do whatever you want because …..

Toby and Mordred: (*speaking simultaneously*) BECAUSE WHO KNOWS WHETHER WE'LL EVEN WAKE UP TOMORROW? LIVE FOR TODAY, THERE'S NOTHING LIKE TODAY, TODAY IS THE FIRST DAY OF THE REST OF YOUR LIFE. IF YOU STAY ON THE SUNNY SIDE OF THE STREET, THINGS WILL NEVER GET SHADY …..

Mordred: We'll teach you all about love, Sunnie! At least the strange, freaky, limited, non-intimate kind of erotic love that we have come to know. If nothing else, we'll advise you on how to fall in love with the idea of love. The fantasy of love is better than no love at all!

Sunnie: (*a harp is being played in the background as Sunnie ponders*) When you speak of love, do you mean participation in the love of the flesh? Of that, I know not much. But I'm willing to learn, and of course, I know that is the way of the brothers of our tribe. And the sooner that I am initiated into the mysteries of their secret society, the sooner that I can start to experience its rapturous exhilaration! (*harp playing stops*).

Mordred: It's not so secret as it used to be, Sunnie. Although your implication has its allure …..

Toby: We ourselves are still unsure as to whether love exists, Sunnie. But should we never know what love is, at least we can enjoy the journey, in attempting to encounter the heart of that mystery. In the pursuit of idealized love, we know that you will undergo carnal experiences that will give you great satisfaction! And a special connection could come along, and heartbreak along with it, but not to worry as …..

Toby and Mordred: (*speaking simultaneously*) CORAZON ROTO IS NEVER A NO NO! PUT A LITTLE LOVE IN YOUR HEART! UP UP AND AWAY IN OUR BEAUTIFUL BALLOON! THIS IS THE DAWNING OF THE AGE OF AQUARIUS!

Sunnie: (*plaintively*) But can you help me find Prince Charming?

Toby and Mordred: (*speaking simultaneously*) Either that, or we'll find you a delightful devil, who'll leave you traumatized for the rest of your days! (*they both laugh wickedly*).

Toby: We'll take you to a sun-drenched island, on the other side of the Eastern Ocean, where all of the Boyropan men go. We'll help you to get over your fear of nudity and relax into hedonistic openness. There's no need for sexual shame, body shame or any kind of shame! We'll teach you how to develop your self-confidence and self-assurance, so that you can negotiate with nefarious hustlers that only want to take advantage of your youth, beauty and privilege.

Toby and Mordred: (*speaking simultaneously*) BECAUSE THERE'S MEN OUT THERE WHO AREN'T DUELING GLINDA THE GOODS LIKE US. YOU'LL KNOW THEM WHEN YOU SEE THEM. YOUR VIOLET SEVENTH CHAKRA SENSE WILL WARN YOU, WE HOPE ….. (*they both break out into hysterical laughter*).

Mordred: We'll accompany you to the Can't Film Festival in Can't, Southern Boyropa. And we'll take you to an underground film festival, that's so much more alternative than Can't, to see movies that are truly cutting edge, made on low-budgets and yet chock full of creativity. Films like *Bast Blanket Bingo* and *Baphomet Beach Party*, starring Aleister Funicello and Anton LaAvalon.

Sunnie: Oh! That would be dreamy! Could you get me a powder blue Princess phone with a direct, twenty-four seven line to Kenneth Anger?

Toby: Why, of course! Whatever you like, Sunnie! We'll give you whatever you want, no questions asked, with our unconditional magnanimity! But before we do anything, we must have your consent: Are you convinced that we have your best interests at heart? Are you on board? Do we have your trust? Are we on the same page?

Sunnie: (*unsure*) I think I'm ready ….. (*with resolve*) I have my doubts, but I want to learn. And regardless of whatever gender I end up adopting for myself, I will never compromise my spiritual beliefs! I could even see having a Third Eye surgically implanted into my forehead! I want it all: the conflicts, the confusion, the decadence, the hangovers, the rejection …..

Toby and Mordred: (*speaking simultaneously*) CHILD, YOU DON'T WANT THE REJECTION! DON'T WASTE YOUR TIME GLAMORIZING PAIN! DON'T SAY THAT WE DIDN'T WARN YOU! AND DON'T YOU DARE SAY THAT WE NEVER DID YOU ANY FAVORS!

Mordred: We hope that you'll trust us and let us lead you to those places that will help you to become the man-woman-thing-type that you truly are! Reflect upon everything that we're proposing carefully. At the same time, don't overthink; don't delay. Advise us of your decision as soon as possible; there's no time to waste, the world could end tomorrow …..

Toby: Exactly, no overthinking, the more quickly that you make up your mind, the sooner that you can get down to the business of having fun! Never forget the words of Auntie Mame:

Toby and Mordred: (*speaking simultaneously*) LIVE, LIVE, LIVE! LIFE IS A BANQUET AND MOST POOR SUCKERS ARE STARVING TO DEATH!

Mordred: HURRY UP, SUNNIE! WAKE UP AND SMELL THE AMYL NITRATE! YOU'VE GOT A LOT OF LIVING TO DO!

Sunnie was intimidated by these foppish leather men. Although he couldn't articulate his impression of them at the time, he later realized that they knew themselves; they knew what they wanted and how to get it. They were comfortable in their own skins and they knew how to laugh their way through adversity. It all seemed so advanced, this world that they were describing; a world that juxtaposed fun and a kind of perversion that Sunnie was barely able to conceive. He was intrigued and his intuition was telling him to take the plunge. Whatever his doubts, he would have to start getting his feet wet. He summoned up his courage; he was ready for his delayed teenage rebellion. It was time for his self-actualization to get underway .....

DATE NIGHT IN JOISEY SHITTY

One night in Nueva Jork, Puta Jork, Amourrica Profunda, when he was thirty-three, Sunnie met a man at the bathhouse. Sunnie and the guy had a sexual encounter that they both enjoyed and the man asked Sunnie if he'd like to get together again. Sunnie said yes, they exchanged phone numbers and then arranged for a date. On a cold winter night, Sunnie took the subway from Nueva Jork to Joisey Shitty across the river. The apartment building where the man lived was difficult to find. To get to the building that he was looking for, he had to go through a hole in a chain link fence and cross a bleak vacant lot strewn with heavy stones. He buzzed the guy's buzzer and the man buzzed him in, without even asking for his name. The guy opened his apartment door and Sunnie immediately knew that something was off. It soon became apparent to Sunnie that the man was very high on some kind of tranquilizer; was he in a K-Hole? The kitchen was blazing with overhead fluorescent light. The apartment's interior was generic and the minimal décor revealed nothing about its tenant; even a cheap motel on the interstate would have had more character. The man disappeared into the bedroom, where a television was blaring at an incredibly high volume. Sunnie followed him, but lingered at the doorway. The man got under the covers and continued to watch an absolutely disgusting D-List horror film. Sunnie tried to talk to him, but none of the man's responses made any sense. This guy had forgotten all about their date. And who knows what kind of riff raff he buzzed into his place; Sunnie didn't want to stick around to find out. So he extracted himself from that bizarre situation. The man didn't even notice that Sunnie had left. Sunnie went back out into the freezing winter night, made his way across the grim vacant lot and then back through the hole in the chain link fence. At that point he was running for the subway and as luck would have it, a train was right there as he raced through the turnstile. He jumped into a seat in the empty subway car and breathed a big sigh of relief. The train pulled out of the station and took him back across the river to home in Nueva Jork.

EL MONSTRUO
OTHERWISE KNOWN AS
UPSTAIRS DOWNSTAIRS

The years flew by. It was now twenty years after his graduation from Mrs. Scheissbook's School for Fascist Piggies and the only thing that Sunnie Deelite had to show for that time was the wreckage of the squandered opportunities of a lost soul. What he had learned to do was how to profit from his looks, which at thirty-eight years of age he wouldn't possess for much longer. What awaited him in his forties? Testosterone injections? A second act in which he'd finally focus on a legitimate career? The Let Go and Let Goddess of Thirteen Step programs and Miyuh Hiyuh Powuh? A safe, vanilla-beige life that would offer him nothing but frustration and loneliness? Once in a while, when the bars, saunas and sex clubs started to bore him, he'd head over to El Monstruo, right off of Krissafuh Street, Nueva Jork.

There are those who would describe it as provincial, yet El Monstruo had its place as a go-to gay / LGBTQ / dance / neighborhood / piano bar. It wasn't the hippest, coolest or trendiest place, yet it was a classic. It was always there when all of the other options had been exhausted. At El Monstruo, the white queens would sing musical comedy numbers by the piano upstairs; the black and Latin queers would dance downstairs. The music that one heard on the dance floor was rarely state of the art or cutting edge. El Monstruo's sensibility tended towards the nostalgic and the sentimental. Disco nights on Thursdays were the highlight of the week. El Monstruo may have been backwater, but at least it wasn't as provincial as Mucha Nieve, Puta Jork, where Sunnie had grown up. In Mucha Nieve, no one drank Beaujolais; they drank *Boojzh-Oh-Lay* ..... *Themmers that was upstate didn't like none of them thar foreignny words in that thar neck of the woods.*

THE NUEVA JORK
THAT SUNNIE DEELITE
NEVER KNEW

..... Once upon a time, the nightlife of Nueva Jork shimmered, during its bleak bankrupt beatnik happening gritty ghetto glam cocaine disco days of the 1960s and 1970s. A Nueva Jorker back then had to have their wits about them, which is not to say that they were incapable of showing some class and treating others with respect. But after Nine-Eleven, the dumbing down and the coarsening of the culture that was taking place throughout Amourrica Profunda came to the city and made its presence known. In street parlance, this new phenomenon was referred to as the "Bro Culture"; in other words, the red state boys who could afford to rent lofts on West Fraudgay for five thousand dollars a month. Nueva Jork had turned into a moneyed refuge for the Bros, who still worshipped a Lower Beast Snide that had died thirty years previously. And even though that formerly bohemian enclave had been gentrified and stripped of its soul, nothing was going to stop The Bros from idealizing its memory and getting their metaphorical punk rock on. Unfortunately, after Nine-Eleven almost all of the alternative venues began to close up shop, especially lesser-known places like the trashy, no-frills Mars Bar. Saddest of all, the Off-Off-Fraudgay and experimental

theatres were being replaced by banks, condo-
miniums, generic pharmacies and suburban-style
department stores .....

ISABELLA GLOUCESTER

Once there was a woman by the name of Isabella Gloucester who'd been raised in Miasma Falls, Puta Jork. On the one hand, she'd never thought about moving away; Miasma Falls was good enough for her and she planned on staying there forever. On the other hand, she knew that she was never going to find love in her hometown. Like so many others, she wanted to be loved; she'd felt this way since she was a little girl. She'd heard that love was a good thing and she wanted it because everyone was always talking about it. Love was the one thing that a person had to have, even if they possessed nothing else, to make their life fulfilling. Her classmates were always joking about sex, since its practice was hidden and in some instances even forbidden. The kids in high school, particularly the girls who were still virgins, were looked upon as prudes; the precocious and sexually active female teenagers were labeled as sluts and whores. A double standard applied to the males, most of whom considered their sexual conquests with females to be nothing more than notches on their belts. As far as Isabella could see, sex had nothing to do with love. Sex was natural yet transgressive, and since sex was inevitably linked to love, was love transgressive as well? How could that be? Love was pure whereas sex was not. In the context of her upbringing, friendships and the streetwise side to life that she adapted herself to as best as she could ….. She didn't see where love fit into the picture.

Despite her inner confusion, Isabella was not to be underestimated. She always had a trick up her sleeve; an ace in the hole. Whenever she failed, she managed to dust herself off, get back onto the horse and ride into the Rust Belt sunset. *Happy Trails* ….. She enjoyed her rose-colored glasses, but as she also relied on her common sense, her realism conflicted with her idealism. Thus she questioned whether she'd be able to find love ….. *WHERE THE FUCK IS LOVE?* ….. She'd often scream out of the windows of her used, maroon Ford Mustang as she did fish tails in the abandoned parking lot of a decrepit teenage wasteland. Weeds growing up through the cracks, broken brown beer bottles and rusty garbage cans; that was reality, whereas love was a mirage. If she was going to find love, she'd better get a move on. She didn't want to end up like the old Crone in her Tarot card deck, the thought of which kept her up nights. She wanted to be the both the Empress and the High Priestess of Tarot. She would chant herself to sleep, repeating to herself over and over: *I VISUALIZE MYSELF AND ACTUALIZE MYSELF AS A PERSON CAPABLE OF BOTH GIVING AND RECEIVING LOVE …..*

Isabella set about making a plan that was designed to work in the cold, cruel world. To this end, she became a Buddhist, or at least she tried to be one. She told herself she would strip away the veil of illusion; she would take on *Maya* as a worthy opponent. But the main reason that she became a Buddhist was to start practicing meditation. She began hanging out in Wurlitzer State Park, by a river full of rapids and a thundering waterfall. She'd sit in the lotus position under a shady tree nearby the riverbank and chant *OM MANI PADME HUM ….. OM NAMAH SHIVAY ….. OM NAMAH SHIVAYA.* Her meditative discipline would help her to realize her dreams and ambitions. Her efforts paid off, as one day shortly after the start of her meditative practice, the Creator presented her with a solution: *GO WEST / GO WEST YOUNG WOMAN / YOUR DESTINY AWAITS YOU.* Isabella knew right then that she must move to Lost Angelist ….. City of love, dreams, fantasy, illusion, ambition, competition, high rollers, winners, losers, predators, smog and suicide. *LOVE / EXCITING AND NEW / COME ABOARD / WE'RE EXPECTING YOU* ….. Love was in Lost Angelist and she was going to get some. Not only would she relocate there; she'd establish herself as a force of nature. She'd transform herself into a sassy, brassy personality who'd find love, or at the very least, attention. Sure, she'd heard about the heartbreak and misery in store for those Lost Angelisteños who'd failed and then faded into obscurity. She'd heard about the ones who'd given up and closed the curtains, to retreat into a past full of bittersweet memories; like the great but long forgotten star of the silent screen, Imogen Havisham. But she would not be discouraged and when she got to Lost Angelist, she wasted no time in getting to work on her one-woman show ….. *as time and tide wait for no man.*

Nothing held her back. So what if she didn't have friends, she'd make some ….. *The Universe provides, the Universe will help me, The Creator will give me what I need and want, I know what I need and want, all I have to do is ask, the Violet Seventh Chakra Goddess will help me to know what love is, and whenever my vessel is empty, the Spirit Goddess will fill it up once again and enable me to enact her works* ….. She became cunning and persistent; that's how she would have to be to create her ideal life. She trusted her intuition and did whatever it took to manifest her career. And little by little, things started happening. Word of mouth got out that Isabella Gloucester had it going on. There were write-ups in the local press, people started coming to see her shows and she developed a following. She became an established performer: an actress who was also a singer, a comedian, a monologist, and most important of all, a businesswoman. She'd escaped the horrible, loveless town of her upbringing; she was living her dream, she was doing it ….. *JUST DO IT, YOU CAN DO IT (AND SHE DID)*. And to top it all off, she finally found the man whose love she would accept as well as reciprocate. He attended one of her shows, they met for a date, they went on a couple of more dates, they got along well, and then they had sex. His name was Flim Philanderer….. For the first few months, everything was working out for the best. But then, Isabella began to be afflicted by creeping doubts. This was more than just paranoia. She loved Flim, but she knew that he didn't love her back. One day, she became very upset and decided that it was time to clear the air …..

Isabella and Flim are standing in the kitchen of Isabella's apartment. The walls of the kitchen are painted semi-gloss white and the space is illuminated by harsh track lighting.

Isabella: *GODDESS DAMN IT! I WANT TO BE LOVED, LOVED, LOVED! LISTEN TO ME AND I'LL TELL YOU WHAT I WANT, I'LL TELL YOU WHAT I NEED ….. EMBRACE MOI, BESAME MUCHO, TOUCHA TOUCHA TOUCHA TOUCH ME, THRILL ME CHILL ME FULFILL ME! CAN YOU ALSO*

BE MY DAYTRIPPER, CREATURE OF THE NIGHT? ….. I don't know how else to say it. But there you have it, that's how I see us, that's my vision of our continued togetherness …..

At first, Flim thought Isabella was being melodramatic, but then he decided to take her seriously. And in that moment, he had to face facts: he didn't love her. He liked her, they were compatible enough; they knew how to not get on each other's nerves. Initially he'd wanted her, but only for sex and after a while that became boring. He liked the idea of love, but the feeling itself wasn't something that he'd ever experienced. *Everyone has an ulterior motive and I've never been a saint* ….. he'd tell himself. Flim knew that she HAD IT: THIS IS THE GIRL, he reminded himself often. She was the IT GIRL and he wanted to be the IT GUY. But that was a fantasy that he used to protect himself from facing the reality of the situation. He'd never known how to be any woman's IT GUY. Being the IT GUY would mean compromising himself and being frustrated; at that point, he'd just have to move on. And so when Isabella told him that she wanted to be *LOVED, LOVED, LOVED*, this is how he responded:

Flim: (*matter of factly*) I'll think about what you're proposing and I'll give you my answer by tomorrow.

Isabella was pissed, but she took him at his word. Maybe she was expecting too much and things would work out better if Flim had some time for reflection. The next evening, as promised, Flim delivered his answer to her.

Flim: I don't love you. I was just in it for the sex. And then that fizzled out. I know that's not enough for you. I've always had a problem with intimacy. I don't know how to get close to you or anybody. And then, you're always working so hard on your career and I figured that if I gave you whatever I could during your spare time, that that would be enough.

Isabella: (*incensed*) You're damn right you have a problem with intimacy! What I'm not getting from you is this: affection. In other words: being held, being hugged and experiencing the warmth of your intimate embrace.

Flim: It just gets monotonous after a while because monogamy is not natural. I've tried my best to keep it exciting, but it's a challenge. By keeping my distance from you, by objectifying you, I maintain a fantasy of who you are, and that's what turns me on. Frankly, I was hoping that you'd get bored too.

Isabella: You're confusing the difference between sex, love and affection. As much as I may dream of being the Earth Mother, who perpetually entraps men within her Bower of Bliss, I'm not so unique. Oh,

I wish it wasn't true! But I know that I'm not alone …..
There are so many women out there, fools like me,
who let themselves get fucked over by opportunistic
creeps like you ….. *LOVE, LOVE, LOVE, HONEY! IT'S
SO MUCH MORE THAN AN F-U-C-K* …..

Flim: I'm sorry, but I just don't know how to give
you what you want and need. If I did, I would. So I'm
done. The drama is a turn-off. Plus, I'm not desperate.

Isabella (*hesitates for a moment, then starts
screaming at the top of her lungs*): MEN MEN MEN! YOU
BASTARDS WITH YOUR PRICKS AND YOUR ONE-TRACK
MINDS! YOU AND YOUR TRICKY DICKS FOR BRAINS! SO
YOU'RE BORED BECAUSE YOU'RE MISSING OUT ON A
CHANCE TO LIVE LIFE AS A LOTHARIO? WOULD IT KILL
YOU TO STROKE ME WITH A GENTLE CARESS! IT ALWAYS
COMES BACK TO THAT REPTILE BRAIN VIOLENCE THAT
INFECTS EVERY CELL OF YOUR TESTOSTERONE-FILLED
CORPOREAL BEING! AT THE END OF THE DAY, IF I'M
LUCKY, ALL I GET IS A WHAM BAM THANK YOU MA'AM!
THE CLASSIC FIFTEEN-MINUTE LAY! AND HERE'S THE
CLINCHER. EVEN IF I'M SO FORTUNATE THAT YOU'VE
NEVER RAPED ME, SEXUALLY ASSAULTED ME OR
EVEN SEXUALLY HARASSED ME: THIS IS MY TIME OF
PERSONAL RECKONING! BECAUSE YOU'VE TREATED
ME LIKE SHIT AND THE PSYCHOLOGICAL DISTRESS HAS
BEEN JUST AS TRAUMATIZING AS EVERYTHING ELSE I
JUST MENTIONED!

Still enraged, Isabella starts throwing, breaking and smashing anything in the kitchen that she can get her hands on: mugs, glasses and dishes. She empties all of the cupboards and starts throwing the contents every which way .....

Flim: (*yelling over the noise of Isabella's tantrum*) Well this is how it's always worked for me, I mean during my disreputable past, during which I was not giving a shit about any of the other women that I've known besides you. If a woman wants to have sex with me, then I know that she loves me. If she doesn't want to have sex with me, then she doesn't love me! And by the way, you're wrong about differentiating between sex, love and affection. They all come together in one package; they're impossible to separate. So if you can't deal with the real world, then how about you go pine away in your Girl Scout slumber party castle in the sky? Because I'm going out to find a woman who can give me a drama-free roll in the hay! That's real, whereas monogamy is just monotheistic brainwashing that keeps the fabric of civilization from ripping apart. And as far as I'm concerned, let it rip apart! The world's being taken over by fascists and fanatics and who knows if we're even going to wake up tomorrow! ..... I'm going to go out and have fun however I want to and I don't care who gets hurt! I'm a fool too, who's ended up being trapped by your possessive bullshit and your limited notions of whatever the fuck love is! I should have told you right from the start that I wanted an open relationship. If I'd done that, I wouldn't even be talking to you right now, because knowing how you are, you would have refused! And I could have avoided wasting my time knowing you! Oh, and one more thing: *WISH ME LUCK WITH MY NEW GIRLFRIEND: POLLY AMORY!*

Flim storms out, slamming the kitchen door behind him. And with each step he takes, he draws closer and closer to the personal hell of his own creation. He turns left onto a dark backstreet, a shortcut that he and Isabella used to frequent in their travels to and fro.

Isabella stands slumped over in the kitchen, staring at the chaos she's created, stunned by what has happened. But then she decides to go out into the night and follow Flim. She knows that the situation is hopeless, but nonetheless she forges ahead, following Flim down the dark backstreet and shouting for him, oblivious to anything outside of her current confusion.

Isabella: (*shining a flashlight ahead of her*) I'm sorry, Flim! Oh my Goddess, I'm sorry! Sorry, Yahweena! Forgive me, Allaheena! Please accept my humblest apologies, Monotheisticka! There's a special Lost Angelist goddess guiding me now; she's a cross between Gypsy Rose Lee and *The Fifty Foot Woman*. The light from her eyes shines through the thickest layers of smog with laser beams that reach all the way to beautiful downtown Burbank. Usually she supports the green light of my truth with green laser beams. But sometimes, like now for instance, she becomes a wrathful deity and her laser beams turn to red. She disapproves of what I've done, for I am a mirthless hypocrite, I am Polly Paradox ….. I have a problem with intimacy too! Who am I to judge, Flim? *COME BACK, FLIM! COME BACK AND WE'LL LAUGH TOGETHER THROUGH THE PAIN!* Intimacy is difficult for everyone, not just men! Who knew that one day we'd be living in a world where loneliness could kill you ….. Conversation has become a dying art since everyone is looking at their Dumbphones all day ….. Just be sugarcoated nice and save all of your vicious behavior for the Internet ….. But the real-life tantrums can't be suppressed and the hissy fits will continue to happen, no matter how hard one tries to prevent them ….. No one talks to anyone and no one talks to me ….. The Starfucks employees behave like paid extras in Stepford Ken And Barbie Westworld ….. No wonder everyone's dropping out, tuning out and turning onto opioids ….. Can you hear me, Flim? Are you there? Oh I don't care, this has to be said, even if you can't hear me, even if you're gone! I'll talk to myself, my polytheistic deities will hear my voice; I have faith in Maya Hiyuh Powuh and these words cannot remain within ….. Oh women and the plight of women! Men will never understand our suffering! To be a woman is to have the blues! (*singing*) BLUE, BLUE, MY WORLD IS BLUE! LOVE IS BLUE! BLUE MEANIES! BLUE HAWAII! BLUE VELVET! BLUE CHRISTMAS! ….. Are you there Flim? Okay it's my fault, I couldn't accept you for being imperfect, I'm such an Oxy-Moron! I'm imperfect, yet I expect perfection ….. What's the name of that school you went to again, Flim? Mrs. Scheissbook's School for Fascist Piggies? (*her speech begins to be punctuated by laughter*) What kind of school would have a name like that? Did Grace Slick, Frank Zappa and Abbie Hoffman collaborate to come up with that monstrous moniker? Love those hippies, they probably think, or thought, that we would have already blasted off from the Blue Green Planet in spaceships and colonized other worlds by this time! Gotta love their idealism! *HA HA! HA HA HA!* A school, with a name like that, is definitely one of the signs of the Apocalypse! Even Auntie Mame would have raised her eyebrows at that one.

Isabella becomes silent and stops in her tracks. She pauses for a moment; her head is hanging down and her flashlight is pointed towards the ground. She takes a few deep breaths. She turns around and starts trudging back home, mumbling and stumbling all the way.

Isabella was enraged and heartbroken but she knew that Flim's leaving her was for the best. She was possessed by the inner life of the classic mid-century housewife. Still, even Betty Draper had more fun than her ..... But she used this romantic disappointment to expand her career even further and in yet another direction. She became the lead singer for a series of Goth bands, each one more successful than the last. She wrote furiously; she burned the midnight oil and she made lemons out of lemonade. Her song, *Goth City*, reached number seven on the Pill-Bored charts; it became a sensation, especially among teenage girls who were living to rebel ..... And to break out of her comfort zone, she composed a poem about *Downton Abbey*, that she described to the press as an exercise in self-expression that was composed merely for her own personal fulfillment ..... Which was not true; she'd written it for the express purpose of expanding her audience by adding cultured, bour-geois, upper-middle- and upper-class women to her demographic. She wanted these women to know that she was more than just a hard-as-nails-claw-your-way-to-the-topper. She wanted these females to see that she was gentle and soft as well .....

ISABELLA GLOUCESTER: CIRRICULUM VITAE

Goth City

From the album *My Happy Trails Are Bittersweet*

Lyrics and music by Isabella Gloucester

We lovey love love cuz I'm a faithful wife
We'll even love each other in the afterlife!
But I could care less if he believes in God
I just want the impact with his sexy bod

Goth City and I'm living the life
Goth City I'm a dominatrix wife
If my guy gets bored and finds some stupid whore
I'll snap my pussy whip and throw him
Out of the door!

Get the hell out of here you piece of trash!
I'll find a faithful guy to fall in love with my ass
I'll keep it sweet and sexy so he'll always be around
He better not mess around out on the town!

Goth City sexy sailor's delight
Goth City where they treat you right!
Goth City laidie takes her kids to school
While another bitch fucks her husband
Out by the pool

I built Goth City and I'm here to stay
I better not discover that you're gay!
Tricky Dick hockey puck slam it in the net
And you better not miss or I'll be very upset!

Goth City and I'm living the life
Goth City I'm a dominatrix wife
I love one guy and I make him apple pie
We're gonna love each other until we die

Oh Downton Abbey!

By Isabella Gloucester

Like a lavender sachet
Like pastel-colored candles
Like pale green cucumber soaps
Like a bergamot oil Earl Grey grande
Like the shadows of sun dappled leaves
Falling across faded postwar pink bathroom tile

Oh Downton Abbey!
How thou doth soothe me!
I am Winnie the Pooh
And thou art my Honey Jar!

Like red wine and Benadryl
Like Quaaludes from days gone by
Or even deadly Diprivan
Your soft murmuring English voices
Transport me like The Sandman
To the Realm of Drowsy Comas

Hurry now! Away!
Downton Abbey awaits!
Never shalt thou sleep more soundly
Having succumbed to its potent inspiration

DORIS AND ARLENE

In high school, Isabella Gloucester had been the member of an Unholie Trynytie with her two best Grrrlfiends at the time, Doris and Arlene. During their association, Isabella started to notice that Doris and Arlene were held back by their inability to channel their creativity into a specific form. The two of them were hopeless, negative victims; quitters who blamed the world for their failures. Eventually, Isabella broke off all contact with that duo. She didn't intend to speak to either one of them ever again.

Then, by means of a grapevine that resurfaced from her past, Isabella heard that Doris had recently won the lottery. Although Isabella had never considered herself to be devious, when she heard that Doris had hit the jackpot, the timing was perfect since Isabella's career was on the skids. People had grown tired of Isabella's bitter, man-hating songs. So she moved back to Miasma Falls with an ulterior motive: to rekindle her fiendship with that rich bitch

Doris. After her return, she discovered that Arlene had become insanely jealous of Doris' lottery win. And so Isabella devised a plan, in which she would use Arlene to gain access to Doris' recently acquired wealth. In this scenario, Isabella cast herself as the leader; Arlene would be the follower. Isabella and Arlene would combine forces and attempt to ruin Doris' life. Isabella would convince Arlene to help her to cook up a plan to extort all of Doris' money. And once she'd acquired the entirety of Doris' assets, she'd skip town with the loot, leaving Arlene with zilch and then going on to establish herself as a Spanish speaking and singing artist in *La Ciudad de México* (she'd been studying Spanish ever since the departure of Flim Philanderer to distract herself from her depression). Isabella had nothing to lose: Amourrica Profunda had deteriorated into a Third World nation and opportunities for advancement in the arts were now few and far between.

However, Isabella's scheme never came to fruition since Doris, never having been a planner, had no idea what she'd do with her newly acquired wealth. She ended up spending it all on gambling trips to Snoregazmya, Nevando in the Western Desert Region. With no interest in attending Thirteen Step meetings such as Casino Anonymous to help contain her self-inflicted crisis, Doris went bankrupt in just three months. When Isabella discovered that

Doris had blown all of the money, she wasn't surprised. She quickly switched gears, deciding to strike up some under-the-table mischief with her ex-flame, Bobby Chooshingoorah. Even if Bobby was a pig and a creep, maybe he'd be flush with cash from his latest jewelry heist. She'd been so naïve with Flim and now it was her time to step out onto the stage as the femme fatale ….. *If I wanted to, I could go and doll myself up, find a banker for a husband, and live in a three million dollar nouveau riche McMansion filled with tacky department store lamps and D list abstract paintings. But at this juncture, especially since I've never been a bourgeois conformist, I think it's time to grow a pair of balls and hit the road. The Goddess of Unorthodox Sexual Liaisons Masquerading As Relationships knows that I was never cut out for the straitjacket of marital non-bliss ….. That would turn me into a castrating bitch! Moreover, Bobby's easy to find: all I have to do is check the wanted posters at the local post office.*

So now Doris and Arlene were back to square one, with nothing to their names except their hair trigger tempers. One night, the two of them were sitting at opposite ends of the bar at their local watering hole, Bad Karma. As usual, they were drunk and were engaged in a heated argument. During this vicious catfight, a reality television producer from Lost Angelist, who'd happened to have grown up in the area and had come back to town for the wedding of a relative, entered the bar. His name was Proteus Frye. He was a man with zero integrity whose sole interest in life was to profit handsomely by exploiting the lowest common denominator, as that symptom of the coarsening of the culture was now expressing itself in the Twilight Lands of the Western World on the Blue Green Planet. He observed Doris and Arlene for a few minutes and fell in love with their odd rapport and their lewd, salacious dialogue. He then stopped their argument to introduce himself; he was known in the industry as a master diplomat and negotiator. Once he'd calmed the girls down, he outlined his plan to transform the two women into reality television stars. Upon hearing Proteus' proposal, both of them fell into a state of hypnotic reverie, hanging onto his every word. Easy street was beckoning to Doris and Arlene from right around the corner .....

BURN BABY BURN
DISCO INFERNO

Isabella Gloucester had moved on; she'd relegated Flim Philanderer to the past. He was a perpetual loser who'd never learn from his mistakes. Once again, the words of Auntie Mame came to mind, whose advice she always followed: *Live, live, live! Life is a banquet and most poor suckers are starving to death!* She looked forward to reconnecting with her blasphemous, belligerent, bellicose bad boy, Bobby Chooshingoorah. For the time being, it made no difference to her whether she was jumping out of the frying pan and into the fire, since as far as she was concerned, drama and dysfunction beat the hell out of being alone. Sure, Isabella and Bobby had had their share of spats. But that didn't mean that they were incapable of having fun!

Isabella located Bobby hitting the slots in Snoregazmya, Nevando. She rescued him from a potential fracas, with some freak called Sunnie Deelite, and whisked him away to a place where they could enjoy a tawdry scene that spoke to their sordid existences ….. Isabella and Bobby porn-key teleported themselves back east to the Outer Bore-Hos of Nueva Jork, Puta Jork, Amourrica Profunda. They were now onstage at the 3001 Ulysses Disco, Questioning Ridge, Puta Jork ….. Dressed in identical white suits, black shirts and black neckties, à la *Saturday Night Fever*, doing disco dance moves that paid homage to that film. In the background, flames leapt up from a line of rusty garbage cans, oxidizing industrial sized containers and corroding Fiats and Volkswagen Beetles. Jagged and twisted metal comprised an installation that had been set up as a temporary shrine to Baphomet. The shrine to Baphomet was frankly too Satanick for Isabella's comfort; her worship of this golden calf took place in her immense closet and she'd planned on keeping that activity a secret forever. But as this was a paid gig and she needed the money, she'd just have to take her chances and hope that the Evilangelists in the crowd would turn a blind eye to her sacrilegious behavior …..

Isabella begins to transform, her face metamorphosing into that of a National Enquirer-style vampire alien baby with fangs and the black eyes of the dramatis personae of "The Devil's Rain". She starts to hiss and speak in Komodo Dragon speech, or what she believes to be Komodo Dragon speech. She then casts a spell on the crowd so that they'll be able to understand her …..

Isabella Gloucester: (*in the lazy, syrupy drawl of a neo-Nazi, Tea Party gal*) I may have a libbeyral-ly-lookin' face, but I'm a Red State Baby at heart! And heartless too, especially when it comes to them thar pro-choice stances and universally health care! NoCare's better! Don't cost no money! It's a simple equation: No Money = No Care! With NoCare, youse gotta pull yerself up by y'alls bootstraps. Y'all can't be lyin' around like some sack of shit diabetic couch potato! Youse better get up and burn some calories. Ain't got no socialist healthcare? No one I know ain't be wantin' no commie care! You'll be fine without it. We ain't no easy street welfare queens waitin' round for another government handout! Remember when Jah-Hee-Zeus were ridin' round with them dinersaurs six thousand years ago? (*crowd whoops and hollers with exuberant enthusiasm*) Why sher ya'll do! Jah-Hee-Zeus is our Evilangelist savior! And that's why we refuse to expose our children to the witchy nonsense of that thar Higher Parterre series! We'll be burnin' up Higher Parterre books tonight in them thar rusty trash-cans! I know some of y'all thinkin': What the hell does *parterre* mean? Is that some bullshit that elitist liber-ally politicians done learned at fancy prep schools?

I ain't certain since mostly I listen to Christian rock (Christianity being the equivalent of Evilangelism Light) ..... I heard tell that *parterre* is some kinda balcony that pipples sit in when they watch the opera. Who the hell can understand opera? It's always in some foreignny language and lotsa classy types that don't like to get they hands dirty goes to watch it ..... *SPRICK INGLYCH, AMOURRICA PROFUNDA'S THE GREATEST COUNTRY IN THE WORLD! YOU CAN'T SPRICK INGLYCH? THEN GET THE FUCK OUTTA MY COUNTRY AND GO BACK TO Y'ALL'S MOSQUITER-RIDDEN ZEEMALAND!*

Isabella starts chanting and the crowd joins in.

WE'RE NUMBER ONE! WE'RE NUMBER ONE! WE'RE NUMBER ONE! WE'RE NUMBER ONE!

Isabella Gloucester: There! I said it four times for each of the Fab Four! Themmers was all right until they said they was more popuhler than Jah-Hee-Zeus ..... You wanna run with my posse, beezotch? Get yourself a monster truck with some six-foot diameter wheels! Them thar Higher Parterre books is so whirly-dervishy and shape-shifty; I won't be truckin' with no wizards and warlocks and that's what themmers is encouragin'! And I don't go to church on Sunday to worship no Allahweenah! I ain't be worshippin' no Yahweenah neither! Excuse my freedom fries, but them ain't the beezotches that I were taught to pray to! Y'all hear me reel good now? Point bein':

We'll burn up some Core-Annes too! We ain't got no limits! No Nazgul-Ringwraith-Death Anorexic is gonna spoil my night of fun! Jes stuff y'alls faces full of Twinkies like nobody's business and pack on them pounds, GRRRL! I sher loved me some Amourrica Profunda, back afore it got all girly and girly manny! All this happened cuz them elitists sprick an Inglych that don't no one I know understand! Them elitists ain't never learned the Dumbspeak, which is how youse make sense to everday folk! Learn the Dumbspeak, you high fallutin' libbeyrally fool!

Them libbeyrals wanna Make Amourrica Profunda Green Again? Hell no! We'll make it black as soot with smoggy cities and dirty streams! I ain't got no passport and a vacation on the banks of the Dead Fish Detergent river's jes' fine by me. Check out them Rust Belt cities and get your Ruin Porn on! Jes' put on yer gas mask, breathe deep and enjoy the scenery. Better watch out fer that dirty brown water comin' outta them drinkin' fountains though ….. And when the Monsanto green grass shrivels up and dies, youse won't have to mow your lawn no more! Fake news made my Jah-Hee-Zeus lovin' brothers and sisters believe that coal is bad! Lies, lies, lies! I love me some coal and I want Sinty Claws to bring me some of them coal shits down my chimnener this December 25th, the day baby Jah-Hee-Zeus were born in a manger that were surrounded by dinersaurs! Ain't no Billary

Benghazi or Jillary Clintonstein gonna tell me what to do! The Dumbspeakers of the Fartland, Amourrica Profunda will rise again! WHOO HOO! PARTAY!

To the delight of the disco patrons, Isabella ends her presentation with an impression of Regan from "The Exorcist". She can do no wrong. She then returns to coordinating dance moves with Bobby Chooshingoorah as "Disco Inferno" plays over and over in the background.

Bobby Chooshingoorah: Hey Isabella! Let's make ghoulish sex tapes for the red states; the people of that demographic worship at the Church of Porn! The Buy-Bull Belt purchases more porn than anywhere else in Amourrica Profunda! We can make a sex tape with a Satanick theme, because you know how those Evilangelists get tired of all the pressure put on them to be good by Jah-Hee-Zeus! They need to cut loose, to transgress and go enjoy some secret Dionysian bacchanals, just like those elitey liberally types they despise so much! And we can even hire some of those *men-who-have-sex-with-men* (who cares if they're gay-for-pay) to make a sex tape. Or even a cissy, sissy girly man tape just to be *contre courant*! And then we can compile a client list, to be made public upon its completion, comprised of highly respected and successful red state males that like to start their gay male relationships in restrooms!

Isabella Gloucester: (*in the lazy, syrupy drawl of a neo-Nazi, Tea Party gal*) Well, I ain't sure about that Bobby! That's sounds like some kind of witchy, warlocky Higher Parterre magick to me! And I must remain strong, never yielding to temptation, for I am a devout follower of Jah-Hee-Zeus, Evilangelism and red-state irrationality! I have both an image and a commitment to my followers to maintain. So if you'll excuse me …..

Isabella breaks away from Bobby to address the crowd and bid her followers farewell.

Isabella: (*in the lazy, syrupy drawl of a neo-Nazi, Tea Party gal*) Goodnight everone! Remember that if youse fall into an irreversible opioid coma, youse ain't got no one to blame but yerselves! Ain't no fault of mine if youse can't pull yerselves away from reality television long enough to get up, go outside and make a differnce in this here hellish world! Y'all better run fast when them tornadies and hurricanies come swirlin' up the pike! Cuz our government ain't got no more money fer none of them natchyral disasters! And by that, I mean our government that I don't want otherwise interferin' with our lives! May Jah-Hee-Zeus save our souls!

And with that, Isabella Gloucester undergoes a reverse transformation, losing the National Enquirer-style vampire alien baby look with fangs and Devil's

Rain black eyes. She dispenses with the Komodo Dragon speech and metamorphoses into a blue state person (her becomes vulnerabibble and then her utters the ultimate impiety) .....

Isabella Gloucester: (*in the enthusiastic up speak of a Valley Girl*) I love my socialist healthcare! You red state people can't intimidate me by calling it commie care! And Jah-Hee-Zeus doesn't exist; Jah-Hee-Zeus is a fairy tale! I wouldn't believe in monotheism even if you paid me to believe in it as a full-time job! Kali-Shiva is my heroine and I adhere to the principles gained from my right-brain immersion within the realm of the Violet Seventh Chakra! (*becoming sentimental*) Violet is close to purple and purple equals blue plus red! Let's all love each other red people and blue people! Red people plus blue people equals purple people!

The crowd gasps and confused murmuring can be heard. Then one wild-eyed fanatic yells out: TRAITOR! Others join in and soon the crowd is chanting wildly as they stomp their feet: TRAITOR, TRAITOR / TRAITOR AND WE HATE HER / NOW I'M A HATER / NOW LET'S ALL BE HATERS / HATERS HATE THE TRAITOR / ISABELLA TRAITOR .....Then a red state girl begins to shout, drowning out the chants of the crowd that then quiets down to listen to her.

Red State Girl: She's just kidding! Lighten up you guys! Everyone knows that Isabella Gloucester put the "E" back in "Evilangelist"! She's been momentarily possessed by the spirits of Billary Benghazi and Jillary Clintonstein. She got spooked by some liberally black magick. You know that this malign influence is everywhere, threatening to infiltrate our red states ….. She's still our heroine!

For a moment, the crowd isn't sure what to believe, but then someone starts laughing and that laughter becomes contagious. Shortly thereafter, everyone is cracking up. Now the crowd is in a good mood again and they get back to their disco dance moves. Because at that moment, all they want to do is PARTAY ….. Isabella and her lack of integrity be damned …..

But Bobby, who couldn't tolerate being overlooked, was feeling resentful towards Isabella for having dissed and ignored him. He stormed out to look for a girl who'd be interested in making a red state pornographick video with him. He'd been under the impression that he and Isabella were about to go on a never-ending road trip, during which they'd live out a series of *Sid and Nancy*-style fantasies while they traversed the dusty landscape of the Western Desert Region. He would always be the rebel; he could not be contained by women like Isabella, whose ambitions were more important than spending time with him ….. Isabella hid her authentic self behind a façade; she wore whatever mask was required to advance her career. In a perfect world, she would have been nude beach, Woodstock hippie, Burning Man free; pagan, polytheistick and polyamorous. But the person that she longed to be was buried under multiple layers of shame. She couldn't even access her shame, because she was ashamed of her shame. In fact, she was ashamed of the shame of her shame. Her shame of her shame of her shame was so deeply entrenched within her being, that she would never be able to rise above it, release it to the outside world and then let it fly free.

BABA YAGA GOES CAMPING

Baba Yaga was relaxing by the creek at the bottom of a ravine in the city of Near-Wanna, in the province of Orckario, in Narniada, a country that lay to the north of Amourrica Profunda. She was taking a well-deserved break after having completed the latest season of her show, *Rock Your World / Cook Your World*. The show was filmed before a live audience; the season's final retro throwback episode featured the preparation of recipes from *The Betty Crocker Cookbook*, 1974. She did not yet know that the show had been cancelled; she'd been outdone and left behind by her former competitors who'd reinvented and repackaged the cooking show format into above-average entertainment. The addition of human-interest stories and interaction with inhabitants of non-Western countries had managed to put a new spin on both the concept and preparation of *haute cuisine*. Besides that, personality had usurped actual cooking skills. As for her female peers, she dismissed them; they were irrelevant to her and she never gave any of them a second thought. She considered them to be as *passé* as home economics teachers from 1950s Amourrica Profunda. She'd been playing hardball with the boys for years; like Maggie Thatcher, she preferred the company of men. She lost no sleep reflecting upon whether she had feminism to thank for the creation of her career. Baba Yaga had always gone after what she'd wanted; she'd aggressively courted fame, money and power. She figured that if she could do it, so could anyone, male or female. The only difference between her and most other people being this: she was the one who'd had the nerve, the one who'd been willing to take the required risks, to make it all happen.

Baba Yaga loved the camera and she knew that she could always depend on the camera. The camera was her best friend and her primary relationship. She looked straight into the lens, using facial expressions that she'd perfected during years of grueling, structured professionalism. *God damn it, everyone knows that I make the best apple pie in any existing multiverse* ..... Yes, she was successful, but her emptiness was profound. She often lay awake at night, in her bedroom whose walls were paneled with cedar and cypress, staring at noirish shadows created by the streetlights outside. That room was but one painstakingly detailed part of one property of her myriad, magnificent real-estate holdings that she used to take refuge from her business empire. But since her work was her life and only her work gave her comfort, she rarely relaxed. She couldn't wait for the next day to begin. It was nights like these, when she realized that she had to return to nature; to heed the call of her inner farmer, gardener and horticulturist. Her only way out of the darkness was to reacquaint herself with *Terra Mater* …..

Baba Yaga: (*facing the camera and speaking Dumbspeak*) Good evenin' my good pipples. Did y'all know that I make a Chocolate Mousse that's to Die-Arrhea For? Or is it Chocolate Moose? Am I spellin' them shits right? Ban Appie-Tit! But afore that, let me tell y'all a little story. One day, I were lyin' down by this here stream all lazy-like, feelin' right guilty that I warn't workin' mah evil fingers to the bone. I were watchin' in the water reel good when this critcher done come swimmin' along. It were a frog; I aimed to make that thar frog my dinner and I sure as hell done that; I caught that thar critcher with my bare hands! ….. When I wants to relax, I jes come on down here and get me a *dharma bum* hobo fire goin' real good and then I catch me somethin'. Case in point: I aim to barbecue this here frog right now! I found me a new kinda happiness after settlin' down on these here banks fer some good livin'! Like the song says: *Give Me The Simple Life* .....

All right, I won't talk like them Deplorabibbles no more ..... (*abandoning Dumbspeak and assuming a cultivated delivery*) Do you remember Alice and Sam from *The Brady Bunch*? Well they've decided to spend the next three months at the Anti-Negative People Spiritual Retreat, hosted by Luchadora Madrugadora, Queen of Stepford Ken And Barbie Westworld. There, they'll dine solely on miso soup, to flush radioactive toxins out of their systems ..... I'm so happy for them! Then they'll dig a hole to Cathay to escape our Not-So-Brave New World. In Cathay, they'll work for a rare earth company, import greenhouses to Western countries that want to decrease their consumption of animal protein and listen to Seventies rock under headphones created by 3D printers. And of course, they'll wear gas masks to protect themselves from the noxious yellow-black smog that continues to proliferate in that land .....

THE DROWSYDAYLE UNDERWORLD

Near-Wanna, Orckario, Narniada was a city of neighborhoods and Drowsydayle was one of its wealthiest. It was located on either side of a gorgeous ravine. During its frequent Siberian winters, when the wind was still, the snow had stopped and the moon and stars shone brightly in the night sky, anyone who happened to be passing through Drowsydayle on foot could not help but be enchanted by its arctic reverie. Foxes could be seen scurrying across its streets or scampering away down its sidewalks ..... Many of Near-Wanna's movers and shakers ended up residing in Drowsydayle's posh, imposing homes. This neighborhood, that was lush and green from May to October, was a sheltered retreat whose inhabitants remained oblivious to the plight of those that lived paycheck to paycheck. Whenever any of the Drowsydaylians were forced to walk down Fugly Street (in Fuglynton, a lower-middle class neighborhood to the southeast of Drowsydayle) they held their noses, looked over their shoulders and made sure that they got themselves out of that locale as soon as they could ..... From November through April in Drowsydayle, most of its properties were decorated with holiday lights; some more luxuriously than others, some with a refined sense of taste and a compelling sense of design. However on the whole, the neighborhood's holiday lights were unoriginal, as they tended to be mass-produced, sterile and soulless ..... Which is not to say that all of the residents of this area were unsentimental. While many of them left their discarded Christmas trees out by the curb on December twenty-sixth, just as many others kept their trees up until after New Year's Day. Some wouldn't even part with their Christmas trees until the end of February ..... And beyond their questionable aesthetics, the holiday lights helped the locals to avoid becoming suicidally depressed.

The median price of a Drowsydayle home was about four million Narniadan dollars. Most of the grand manors in this neighborhood had been built in the following architectural styles: Georgian, Edwardian and Victorian. If one were to peek inside the windows of these mansions, one could quickly surmise from the overabundance of tacky department store lamps and D-list abstract paintings adorning many of the walls ..... That money can't buy taste. The majority of these homes were painted in somber gray, brown or black. The inside lights of these manors were usually extinguished after eleven o'clock in the evening, since the neighborhood was filled with early-rising professionals. And while certain of these mansions were perpetually shrouded in dark shadows, the exteriors of others were excessively accentuated with harsh floodlights. Which were presumably used to provide the homes with a touch of class, but which ended up making them look like locations for horror films. Some of the owners were purposely absent, as they traveled frequently or lived in foreign countries. Many of the manors functioned as ever-appreciating real estate investments, since Near-Wanna was known to be an up and coming city, whose population was increasing by approximately one hundred thousand inhabitants per year. Looking southward over the tops of the trees, the skyscrapers of the *Blade Runner Meets The Brady Bunch* downtown were visible from this Not-So-Sure-Would Forest .....

The Piney Woods Group, also known as The Pineys, were a motley crew of abandoned Christmas tree appropriators. They'd start cruising through Drowsydayle on December twenty-seventh, to pick up all of the Christmas trees that had been left out by the street. The Pineys lived for those moments when they could warm themselves by the light of gigantic, crackling bonfires. If they'd had their way, the Pineys would have started their *feux de joie* at the bottom of the Drowsydayle ravine. They had to forgo that pleasure however, since Near-Wanna was a city whose rules were strictly enforced. The burning of bonfires down in the ravine would definitely come to the attention of the local police, who regularly patrolled Drowsydayle. Bonfires qualified as a threat to public safety and were therefore illegal. Truth be told, the police were often bored at night and enjoyed cruising through well-to-do Near-Wannian neighborhoods, looking for potential delinquents they could arrest for being in the wrong place at the wrong time. It didn't take much for one to stand out as being subversive in this neighborhood, as golf was its preferred sport ..... With these factors in mind and because the Pineys also prided themselves on being discreet, they preferred to build their pyres in the absolute secrecy of the dark, evergreen forests of Northern Orckario. Over the years, the Pineys had developed the following ritual: They stuffed all of the abandoned Christmas trees into the vans of their convoy. They would then drive seven hours north-west, to the town of Rune, to visit a flat, dry clearing, where they'd be unobserved by anything but wild-life. They always drove slowly when going up north to avoid potentially fatal crashes involving moose that often emerged from the woods to cross the roads.

The Pineys had just finished stuffing all of the abandoned Christmas trees into their vans, when they heard a clamor originating from a southerly direction. A noisy rabble was approaching. The sound of loud, drunken voices and harsh laughter drew closer. Stainless steel pans were being banged upon with large metal soupspoons, spatulas and whisks. And then the source of this brouhaha and the figures involved appeared: it was a group of about three hundred trespassers who were wearing industrial strength, stainless steel necklaces that were attached to flashlights. The flashlights were positioned on the necklaces so that their light was shining up into the faces of the intruders. It was a streetwise-looking gang that was the opposite of nine to five. Their faces were made up in clown white; their lips and eyes were done up with red and black makeup. Some were dressed in casual street wear or gym outfits while others were attired as if for a Halloween parade. But whatever they were wearing, they were unified in their purpose. Yes, it was a horde of clowns that was approaching. They'd become telepathically aware of the presence of the discarded Christmas trees and were bent upon their destruction. They'd brought flamethrowers along with them to eradicate as many abandoned trees as possible. The clowns were signaling, to anyone who happened to witness them, that pagan tribalism had returned; that monotheism had finally crashed and burned. The entire scenario resembled an ancient ritual from the dark ages ..... And it was not just the clowns who were determined to destroy the Christmas trees. There were other beings waiting in the wings for their chance to wreak havoc as well. Just a short distance away, zombies were tearing up the soil and clawing their way out of the ground, down by the creek that snaked through the Drowsydayle ravine. Werewolves were snarling in the shadows and steampunk mercenaries, holding umbrellas over their heads, came floating down from the sky. The wardrobe of the latter resembled a hybrid of *Dune, Mary Poppins* and *Twenty Thousand Leagues Under The Sea*.

And then Baba Yaga showed up, bursting through a hole in the bank of the stream at the bottom of the ravine. She was now stomping up the slope of the gorge and heading towards Drowsydayle. She was a giant, covered with dirt and vines and her eyes bulged out of her head. She had no patience for clowns, zombies or werewolf devotees; she was a predator, she acted as an elemental force and her appetite needed to be satiated. As she sprinted up the slope at lightning speed, she wasted no time in creating mayhem. She tore through the fancy mansions with her merciless iron claws, throwing them to the left and to the right of her. Any residents, who were unlucky enough to have been home at the time were hurled by Baba Yaga up into the air. When they looked appetizing enough, she hastily consumed these unfortunates as hors d'oeuvres. Once she'd destroyed enough manors to momentarily satisfy her lust for destruction, she started digging holes at the bottom of their foundations. Her digging took place at such an incredible velocity that within the space of a few minutes she'd reached the molten iron inner core of the Blue Green Planet. The temperature of the inner core was hotter than the surface of BGP's sun. Light, heat and fire shot up through all of the tunnels that Baba Yaga had created. The surrounding terrain was now pockmarked with emerging volcanoes and molten lava was overrunning the landscape.

Some of the residents of Drowsydayle, especially those who felt stultified by their riches, were undergoing an awakening as a result of the clear and present danger that they now faced. Even though they were afraid, for once in their lives they were aware of something else besides the humdrum, mundane and banal quality of their everyday existences. They'd been shaken out of their gentrified, petrified comas. No matter how hard they tried to be respectable members of their community, the creative spark was missing. Because they were always doing what they should be doing, what they were supposed to be doing ….. Instead of what they truly wanted to be doing. The Near-Wannians as a whole were subject to tremendous peer pressure; their culture expected them to conform to its dictates. But living like this was too much to take and as a consequence, within the confines of their luxurious neighborhood, the opioid crisis was in full bloom ….. In that moment, they realized that they could live with less and would be happier if they chose to downsize. But it was too late for that. Baba Yaga shrieked as the Drowsydaylians were being annihilated by explosions of heat and fire. And although they'd wanted the best for their children, teaching them to be as empathetic and compassionate as possible ….. Mother Nature was a cruel taskmistress, amoral and irrational. And it made no difference to Baba Yaga that the Drowsydaylians had chosen to sleepwalk through life in a delusion of morally superior goodness ….. The nearby ravine quickly filled to the brim with lava that flowed at such a high speed, as well as volume, that it spread out like a multidirectional tsunami and eventually covered most of the city. Few escaped and the population of Near-Wanna was decimated.

THE EVOLUTION
OF ISOLAMICKA

..... Once upon a time, there was a land called Amourrica Profunda ("AP") that was considered to be one of the most enlightened and progressive countries on the Blue Green Planet ("BGP"). Its coasts bordered the Eastern and Western Oceans; to the north lay Narniada; to the south was Immigrador. Amourrica Profunda, Narniada and Immigrador were all part of a massive supercontinent called *Pangolina*. In the year 5950, the Evilangelists in AP's Fartland began to officially promote their anti-intellectual conception of existence. That's when everything started to unravel, when the nation began to lose its precious integrity, by selling its soul to the highest bidder .....

..... The Evilangelists believed that six thousand years in the past, Jah-Hee-Zeus ("JHZ") had suddenly, and randomly, appeared in the darkness of

Nothingness, also known as *Le Néant*. The exact origin of JHZ remains unknown to this day. The Evilangelists considered both the birth of JHZ, and his creation of the cosmos, to be unfathomable events of great spiritual consequence. According to Evilangelist mythology, JHZ created all of the multiverses, including the Universe in which the Androgynous and Galatea galaxies and the Via Lactea are found. After all of the aforementioned was in place, JHZ created the Blue Green Planet. The date of BGP's creation is referred to by the Evilangelists as *Year Zero*. At first the planet was square, but after about two thousand years, it had morphed into a spherical shape, as the result of wear and tear inflicted upon it by comets, asteroids, the Sun and the Moon. JHZ created all of BGP's flora and fauna, including gargantuan reptiles called *dinersaurs*. JHZ then created the first humans; the original humans lived in an ancient region of Immigrador called *Mesoamourrica*. As the planet's human population grew, it began to disperse and eventually settled all of BGP's available land space ….. In the year 3000, a series of devastating earthquakes split Pangolina into seven smaller continents. Many lives were lost; the dinersaurs became extinct, but their reptile relatives (crocodiles, lizards, turtles, snakes and birds) survived. The human population quickly rebounded and BGP's flora and fauna continued to proliferate …..

Two thousand and five hundred years later, in the year 5500, Amourrica Profunda ("AP") was discovered by explorers from Illuminata, a multi-lingual continent whose Western Zone bordered the Eastern Ocean. AP's first settlement, *Fuente de la Juventud*, was founded in 5505; in 5510, AP's first state, *Orlando*, was created. In 5515, Fuente de la Juventud was established as the capital city of Orlando; in 5520, Fuente de la Juventud became the capital city of all of AP as well ….. In 5605, *The Fraternity of Fickle Founders* of AP created and then adopted *The Declaration of Hypocrisy*, which established and proclaimed AP to be a sovereign nation. By this time, AP was comprised of fifty-two states (the same number of states as the number of weeks in one year of the Gregorian calendar) that had been officially incorporated into The Republic of AP. In 5606, an official document entitled *The Confirmation of Colonial Release* was shipped across the Eastern Ocean to Fuente de la Juventud, Orlando, AP. This document was created by the High Council of Illuminata, who were based in Bruschetta, the capital city of both the country of Dunkelstein and the continent of Illuminata. With The Confirmation of Colonial Release, Illuminata recognized the legitimacy of the autonomous nation of AP. The Illuminatians had become incredibly wealthy from their colonization of the rest of BGP, through the acquisition of treasures and resources, seized from lands that they'd been subjugating for over one hundred years. Therefore, they had no need for AP's goods and services. And so all ties with Illuminata were broken, as that continent determined that no profit was to be made through trade with Amourrica Profunda. The Illuminatians also maintained a condescending attitude towards the refugees who'd abandoned Illuminata for AP; those émigrés were considered to be repressed, hysterical and obsessed with religion. The High Council of Illuminata ended the text of The Confirmation of Colonial Release unceremoniously with the following words: BE GONE. WE RELEASE YOU. GOOD LUCK AND GOOD RIDDANCE. P.S. DON'T CALL OR WRITE. After that point, AP thrived for the next 300 years .....

By the year 5950, Amourrica Profunda was already deteriorating and the country's sterling reputation, around the world, had become severely tarnished. AP had been established as a democracy, but from the outset, The Fraternity of Fickle Founders had had their fingers crossed. Because they knew that since the beginning of recorded history, democracies had tended to devolve into autocracies, oligarchies and plutocracies. Due to this decline of the formerly civilized nation of AP, the great republics of BGP, as well fifty percent of the Amourrica Profundans themselves, began to refer to AP as *Mourrzicka*. In 5955, the name of the nation of Amourrica Profunda was officially changed to Mourrzicka, since seventy-five percent of the population of the country could no longer correctly pronounce the name Amourrica Profunda ….. In 5960, the entire state of Orlando, including Fuente de la Juventud, was decimated by an outbreak of Zeema, a fatal disease carried by mosquitoes that had originated in the country of Naambyaah, on the western coast of the tropical continent of Gowaandaah. Over the next few years, casualties mounted and as a result of this major loss to its population, the state's infrastructure disintegrated and it became ungovernable. Thus in 5965, *Voldemordor* (located in the state of Venerea, on the Central Eastern Coast) became Mourrzicka's new capital city.

In 5980, a flamboyant trillionaire by the name of Turmerico Inflammatorio rose up within the ranks of Mourrzicka's decaying political system, to become *the voice of untruth*, since he only told his followers *what they wanted to hear* ….. In 5985, he was elected mayor of Nueva Jork, Puta Jork (a megalopolis with fifteen million inhabitants, located in Mourrzicka's Northeastern Zone). In 5990, he was voted in as the governor of the state of Puta Jork, Northeastern Zone, Mourrzicka ….. His ruling technique involved distracting the populace by engineering chaos and drama, which he achieved by creating an ongoing political theater that was covered by every available media outlet. His methods included making wildly contradictory statements and fomenting controversial disruption among friends and foes alike. Turmerico was incapable of rational thinking; the entirety of his thought process originated in his reptile brain. His reasoning tended to be rigid and compulsive. He had no sense of shame or decency; he was incapable of restraining himself in any way. The Mourrzickans suspected that he didn't even know the difference between right and wrong. Although Turmerico was raising the population's collective blood pressure by making impulsive decisions with geopolitical consequences (as a result of his highly unstable nature) he inspired their fascination nonetheless; they fell under the spell of his anti-charisma. The inhabitants of the capital city of Voldemordor, however, had never been fooled by Inflammatorio's con artistry and became incensed by the way that he was leading the nation down the road to ruin. The best and the brightest had always been drawn to Voldemordor. Eventually, its inhabitants realized that they could function on their own; they no longer needed to be a part of Mourrzicka.

And so in early 5995 Voldemordor, and its population of ten million, voted to secede from Mourrzicka to become its own separate city-state. Six months later, the secession was finalized. Thanks to the brilliance of its scientists, engineers and architects, a dome-forcefield was constructed, that by early

5996 covered the entire city-state to keep out all of the Mourrzickans (who were now referred to by the Voldemordorians as *Isolamickans*). In 5998, the name of the nation of Mourrzicka was officially changed (once again) to Isolamicka, as seventy-five percent of the population now considered their country to be superior to all of the other nations of BGP. Three-quarters of the Isolamickans hated Voldemordor and its elitist population; they vowed to one day attack, sack and destroy that city. With Voldemordor under their control, the Isolamickans could return to *The Good Old Days*; in other words, the time before AP had deteriorated (and morphed into Mourrzicka and then Isolamicka) ….. Tumerico Inflammatorio seized control of Isolamicka, by means of a bloodless coup, one week after the secession of Voldemordor. The coup was easy to achieve, since Turmerico was now unconditionally supported by seventy five per-cent of the Isolamickans. Inflammatorio's lieutenant governor, Shame-Based Shelley Shamway, took over as governor of Puta Jork and Turmerico established the seat of his new regime in Branighan, in the state of Missoolah (located in the Confederate Region of Isolamicka). Branighan, Isolamicka's new capital city, lay just five miles north of the border between Missoolah and the state of Archaicka.

THE DEEPER MEANING
OF SMORES

Meanwhile, somewhere in the landlocked state of Missoolah deep in the heart of Isolamicka ….. *it were night in them thar piney woods.* A television was playing at low volume in the living room of a trailer; in the kitchen, there was a light on above the stove. The rest of the trailer was dark. A family was sitting down to dinner, with their elbows on the kitchen table. They sat in silence. Their hands were clutching their forks and knives tightly; their cutlery was pointed upwards. They started to chant loudly as they pounded the bottoms of their clenched fists on the white Formica table …..

MORE SMORES PIE! SMORES PIE FOR LIFE! SMORES PIE IS LIFE! SMORES PIE IS THE LIFE! SMORES PIE EVERY DAY! SMORES PIE EVERY NIGHT! SMORES PIE SWEET AND NICE! FUCK THAT PUMPKIN SPICE! SMORES PIE ALL THE TIME! SMORES PIE AIN'T NO CRIME! SMORES PIE OUTER SPACE! TIME TO WIN THE RACE!

They stopped chanting, continued pounding in silence for about thirty seconds and then came to an abrupt halt. A twelve-year old boy named Bobby stood up. He was wise beyond his years and he began to speak loudly:

Bobby: If only usns could experience the fun times resultin' from the daily consumption of Smores pie! And we'd stuff our faces with Smores pie every night too! If only usns could wolf down them Smores pies to our hearts content, without anyone ever sayin' stop, that's too much, you've had enough now! There wouldn't be no bigly government controls to keep usns from blowin' up as big as McMansions if that's what usns wanted! There wouldn't be no Naambyaah state to keep usns from partakin' of sweet sugary sodas, if that's what constituted usns vision of a good life like the ones that's illustrated on the Jehovah's Witnesses *Watchtower* magazine covers!

Bobby stopped speaking. He sat down and assumed the position required for pounding and chanting with the forks and knives. There was another moment of silence. Everyone assembled looked straight ahead with serious looks on their faces. They started pounding the bottoms of their fists, with their cutlery pointed upwards, on the white Formica table once more ..... Then one of them started to giggle. However, when engaging in this ritual, giggling was forbidden. So at that point, Big Mama, a woman who was known throughout the entire county as some-one not to be messed with ….. Made a harsh shush-ing sound …. SHOOOOOOSH! They then resumed their pounding and loud chanting with grim looks on their faces as before.

   ….. *This was how the group, with their combined focus on chanting and pounding, controlled the zombies. With every three slams of the bottoms of their fists, forks and knives, a new zombie awoke from its pod in a zombie greenhouse. Zombie patrols would then rise up and search out riches wherever they were hidden or buried. The spoils would then be repossessed and delivered straightaway to the Center for the Reappropriation of Valuables in Branighan, Missoolah. Control of the zombies origi-nated from within a vast network of Isolamickan groups, seated at tables across the Fartland in this manner. This practice had been going on for years in various clubs and associations who met regularly in the Fartland's Evilangelist churches. It was not yet known how these groups, by performing these ritu-als, managed to control the zombies in this way …..*

   Once again, Big Mama motioned everyone seated at the table to stop the pounding and chant-ing. They became silent, put down their forks and knives, folded their hands on the table in front of them and stared straight ahead. Big Mama got up from her chair and turned around to open the trailer door. She stood at the top of the small aluminum staircase, at the entrance to the trailer, sniffing the air and looking up at the sky. She turned off the floodlight that illuminated the property and let her eyes adjust to the darkness. It was a clear night and a carpet of brilliant stars gradually became visible overhead (streetlights in this rural area were rare as tax revenue to fund the local infrastructure had been diverted to wealthier parts of the state). Fortunately, the entire populace was armed to the teeth and was perfectly capable of dispensing with any thieves, robbers and ruffians on their own, without the help of any bigly government.....

Big Mama motions to Bobby. He comes to the door and stands beside her. She places her hand on his shoulder.

Big Mama: Bobby, yer gonna go over thar to that thar waarhouse and check in on our zomber friends? To make sher themmers is growin' up reel good in they pods, all right? Come on right back now and let me know if the latest batcha them critchers be hatched out and ready to go along pillagin' and plunderin'.

Bobby: Oh yes Big Mama, I'm goin' over thar right now! I sher as hell can't wait to go check up on them thar zombers! Them critchers was growin up right fine last time I checked!

Big Mama continues to keep her hand placed on Bobby's shoulder as they stand in the open trailer doorway. And then ever so gradually, Big Mama's pupils and irises, as well as the whites of her eyes ….. Turn pitch black. As the two of them stare out into the darkness, Bobby's pupils and irises, as well as the whites of his eyes become coal black. But Big Mama's eyes are so much more frightening, because she is *The Death Mother*, to whom the zombies will remain loyal for as long as she exists …..

Zombie Picnic

The Zombie found a clearing in a thicket by the side of the road. Here he'd take shelter for the night. He settled down into a pile of leaves and fell asleep to dream of better days when the pickings had not been so slim …..

….. A suburban couple is sitting on a red and white checked tablecloth by a creek having a picnic. Aided by the creeping skills of a highly efficient predator, a gentle Zombie appears without notice. He looks passive, non-threatening and is blessed with chartreuse-colored skin. He hesitates, not being sure whether he's welcome. The couple has no fear of him; in fact, the Mrs. has surmised that he's a vegan and that he practices transcendental meditation …..

The Mrs: Oh c'mon, hubbie! Don't be a spoilsport! Let's invite him over. Don't you want to meet some new people? You never want to meet any new people! Well, I'm fed up with you! You stuffed shirt ….. You're such a party pooper! Oh you! I've just about had it with you! You're going to meet some new people whether you like it or not! Man is a social animal, after all …..

She beckons to the green zombie. He approaches the couple, and then in a flash and a whirl, the Zombie proceeds to consume the Mr. and the Mrs. with the ferocity of a shark. Before she starts convulsing and lapses into unconsciousness, the Mrs. thinks: *Could there be a good way to think about my death?* But the time for philosophizing has past and the light of the Blue Green Planet sky fades quickly from her view ….. After he finishes feasting on the couple's corpses, the chartreuse zombie regains his composure, washes himself off in the brook and then sits down serenely on the red and white checked tablecloth. He assumes the lotus position and focuses on his ingoing and outgoing breath. After completing his meditation, the Zombie proceeds with his journey. He comes to a fork in the road. *I sher am tired of livin round all of them rich pipples in Drowsydayle,* he says. *I wants to be round folks that ain't got no shame of bein' devoured.* He has two choices as to how he can proceed: to the right lies Narniada;

to the left Isolamicka. The Zombie veers to the left, because while the Narniadan culture remains human and humane in most ways, in Isolamicka he can enjoy having his reptile brain stimulated by the ongoing conflict and chaos that has overtaken that country. To live in Isolamicka is to live by pillage and plunder, which the Zombie looks forward to ….. As he's greedy, primitive and lusting after destruction.

UNDER THE DOME

Isolamicka had deteriorated into a nightmare of squalor, skirmishes and instability. Fortunately, the Voldemordorians lived in relative safety under a forcefield bubble that the Isolamickans referred to as *The Dome*. The Voldemordorians were a delightful yet surprisingly tenacious people who possessed superior means of communication. Their language was called Smartspeak. The mayor-governor of Voldemordor was Ebenezer Prosecco. He managed the day-to-day operations of the city-state. His wife Elizabeth Prosecco governed with equal power by his side ….. In Voldemordor, the population had undergone a process of accelerated evolution, facilitated by advances made by research scientists whose work was supported by the Voldemordorian government. Thanks to these developments, the sexes now resembled one another more closely. The men had vaginas for eyes and the women had penises for noses. Although the anus remained in both sexes, both males and females now possessed an orifice in the groin that was used solely for urination; it was located where the genitals had once been found. Sexual activity now occurred by means of the face; in less-civilized cultures, this would have been referred to as *face-fucking*. But Voldemordorian societal mores discouraged their people from using any vocabulary that referenced genitalia in a non-clinical way. Therefore, the politically correct term for face-fucking was *tactile symbiosis*.

Inside the The Dome, everything was warm and fuzzy, touchy feely, teddy bears, puppies, kittens, glitter, cupcakes, confetti, party hats and sparklers. The influence of *Hello Kitty* predominated the cityscape. Smiles, giggles and contentment ruled the day, as none of the people lacked for either money or comfort. The Voldemordorians dressed in elaborate hooded capes of pink and blue and spent their abundant leisure time shopping for mood-enhancing lamps and decorative objects to brighten up their dwelling spaces, which resembled those of the original Star Trek Enterprise (*Star Trek*, 1966-1969). In the home, time was set aside everyday to meditate; one chanted *OM MANI PADME HUM, OM NAMAH SHIVAY* and *OM NAMAH SHIVAYA*. In Voldemordor, all subcultures, racial minorities, immigrants, gender distinctions and sexual orientations were welcomed unconditionally. Upon the arrival of any prospective resident, assistance was provided to help them to settle in, integrate themselves into the culture and become productive citizens ….. That being the case, not everything was sunshine, lollipops and roses Under The Dome. Even though their forcefield bubble served to protect them, the Voldemordorians lived in fear of the Isolamickans, and the turmoil that they barely survived in outside of The Dome. Beyond the sanctuary of The Dome lay a minefield of guns, meth labs, toxic black sludge, unlit roads, massacres and roving bands of crazed Evilangelists, who lived to praise their savior, Jah-Hee-Zeus. One half of the Isolamickan population would never believe in any other deity; to do so would condemn them to infernal damnation in the afterlife. The other half of the populace had become skeptical of monotheism. They preferred earthy gods, like Baphomet, who they worshipped and called upon to help them to deal with pressing matters related to their everyday existences.

These were desperate times for the Isolamickans and they'd become rough around the edges. They remained a spirited bunch, but they struggled to contain their rage; the harshness of their everyday lives forced them to be wary even of their own countrymen. An elaborate system of codes and discreet hand gestures had evolved to help the Isolamickans distinguish between friend, foe or frienemy. But the codes had to be updated constantly, as a signifi-cant minority functioned as double agents with ties to Voldemordor ….. Often at night, the Isolamickans set huge bonfires alight in downtown squares or alongside the rivers and ports of their cities. They would then participate in sing-alongs (actually *scream-alongs*) that they'd come to believe would keep the dark forces at bay. This expression of their shared humanity made them feel alive and gave them hope. The people would gather at massive *Mad Max*-style karaoke events and release their frustrations by shrieking themselves hoarse to clas-sic grunge, hard rock and heavy metal power bal-lads (previously outmoded styles of music that had come back into fashion). Musical gatherings such as these helped the Isolamickans to retain their sense of the sacred.

The current president of Isolamicka was Turmerico Inflammatorio. He ruled Isolamicka from a pal-ace full of golden toilets in magnificent Branighan, Missoolah. The motto of this city was *Ugly Is The New Beauty*; its preferred style of architecture was *Brutalism*. By Inflammatorio's side stood his stern and commanding wife, Curcuma Moulu. She functioned as a Lady Macbeth for her husband; she encour-aged him to go ahead with the most ambitious and dastardly of his plans. Tumerico also maintained a relationship with a mistress, who went by the name of Pornie Damnsell. Curcuma was aware of the situation occurring between Turmerico and Pornie and she wasn't happy about it. She tolerated it however, as their marriage had always been one of convenience and she didn't want to risk losing the assets she'd gained through her matrimonial alliance with Turmerico. Besides, Curcuma was open-minded and saw no point in depriving herself of the opportunity to engage in her own extra-marital affairs from time to time …..

It was Turmerico's dream to rule Voldemordor, as well as Isolamicka. But he would not be able to achieve that goal until he learned Smartspeak, Voldemordor's official language. Smartspeak was a complicated tongue that confounded many. Its pronunciation was difficult and its grammar was exceedingly complex. It was also a language based on positive intentions. On the other hand, Dumbspeak (Isolamicka's official language) was Neanderthal by comparison; a base and primitive tongue that was the easiest language to learn on the entire Blue Green Planet. Naturally, the Voldemordorians were fluent in Dumbspeak ….. To conquer Voldemordor, Turmerico would have to learn Smartspeak to the best of his ability. Beyond that, a team of interpreters, translators and linguistic code breakers would be required. Otherwise, the exact method for penetrating Voldemordor's forcefield bubble would never be known. Becoming proficient in Smartspeak would not be an easy task for Turmerico, who was not equipped with the exacting discipline, organizational skills or intellectual curiosity necessary for such a weighty matter. Fortunately, Curcuma drove and hounded him incessantly, exhorting him on a daily basis to focus on this undertaking.

And then one day, after having spent hundreds of hours with a multitude of linguistic experts and language professors, as well as having been treated with a course of anti-lobotomy drugs to expand and improve his limited cranial capacity, Turmerico Inflammatorio finally achieved semi-fluency in Smartspeak. He then arranged for a small army to break through the Voldemordorian forcefield bubble. Three evil scientists, who'd recently been exiled from Voldemordor for having maintained treasonous connections with Isolamicka, were hired by Turmerico to assist with this endeavor. After finally cracking the code that would enable them to penetrate the forcefield bubble, the evil scientists were then able to pornkey teleport Isolamickan troops into Voldemordor. Once the infantry had gained access in this way, they took control by means of a very clever method; the soldiers disguised themselves as gentle, adorable clowns, dressed in primary colors, wearing red noses, carrying bunches of pastel colored balloons and smiling sweetly. The Voldemordorians were instantly charmed ….. Psychiatric experts operating under Inflammatorio's command had also learned through their research that the Voldemordorians were partial to the colors pink and blue. Pink and blue rendered them docile and regrettably, vulnerable as well. For this reason, the troops distributed pink and blue candies to all of the Voldemordorians; these candies contained mind-altering drugs. Strict supervision of the city-state's inhabitants commenced at this point, to make sure that they took their medication every day. Once the candies had taken effect, the entire populace was then subject to mind control by teams of Isolamickan hypnotherapists.

The subjugation of the Voldemordorians by Turmerico Inflammatorio's enforcers was now complete. They dutifully took their pink and blue candies every day that kept them cooperative, amenable and malleable. However, the Voldemordorians had always been blessed with an intelligence that was innately superior to that of the Isolamickans. Unbeknownst to their Isolamickan conquerors, they also possessed the ability to communicate with each other via mental telepathy. An increasing number of Voldemordorians realized that the pink and blue candies were keeping them submissive, compliant and obedient. Silent messages containing warnings about the dangers of the pink and blue candies began to circulate among the population via telepathic mind linking and subliminal networking. In time, those messages were distilled into a single dispatch, created with the intention of inciting a rebel movement:

Flush the pink and blue candies down the drains and toilets! In this way, their potency will be diluted by the salinity of the Eastern Ocean. Sadly, some of our fellow Voldemordorians will fall under, and remain under, the influence of the candies, perhaps never returning to us as a consequence of that dependency. Some of our people have been seduced by an element that we have in common with the Isolamickans ….. That being the violent and primitive power of the reptile brain. The reptile brain is an ancient aspect of our species' physiology and even the best and brightest among us struggle to resist its power. In any case, flushing the pink and blue candies is the only way for our people to not only survive, but to flourish.

Penelope the Pantone Princess, Leader of the Voldemordorian Resistance, composed the following anthem for their movement:

Down With Pink And Blue

Flush the pink and blue
It's not good for you!
Flush the drugs away
Don't do what they say

Channel all your thoughts
We cannot be bought
We are coming back
Ready to attack

We have not been conquered
Power will be ours
We were feeling bonkers
Now we see the stars

Every thought they're thinking
We can understand
We are on a mission
Fate will guide our hand

And Vindicktivio Vulckanmonger, the Leader of
the Isolamickan Enforcers (who remained wary
of the captive Voldemordorians) composed an
Isolamickan anthem dedicated to the continued
suppression of Voldemordor:

You Can Run But You Can't Hide

Time is running out!
You will hear us shout!
If you escape your bubble
We will give you trouble!

See now how we frown?
You will all go down!
We will all get lit!
You will all get hit!

So dream now of the good times
You had when you were young
We're going to come and get you
It won't be any fun!

The forcefield will not save you
The bubble will deflate
Take care it won't be long now
Before you meet your fate!

LIFE ON PLANET GORP

Planet Gorp was a totally gorp world. And the people of that world loved to make dream catchers. No one was worried about motivation, man. No one worked for the man. Each of the inhabitants had their own self-sustaining business that contributed to the wellbeing and maintenance of their community. The Gorpians' way of living was based upon philosophies espoused in an episode of the original *Star Trek* television series entitled *Whom Gods Destroy*. Recreational drug use was encouraged and whatever they got high on they shared, greed being a rarity on this world where hoarding rarely occurred. The Gorpians were mellow and not prone to anger. Anger was frowned upon and all inhabitants were encouraged to practice meditation, to help them to develop the mindfulness necessary to resolve their conflicts rationally. Everyone was emboldened to be Zen and present; to *BE HERE NOW*. The Gorpians would often remind each other to stay grounded, breathe and let go. Envy, jealousy, judgment, insecurity and the need to be competitive were discouraged. One of the most respected tribal leaders, who was known as Anna Thesia, explained the Gorpian philosophy as follows:

Anna Thesia: EVERY ONE OF YOU IS A BEAUTIFUL FLOWER AND THE ONLY THING YOU HAVE TO DO TO FULLY REALIZE THE UNLIMITED POTENTIAL OF YOUR INFINITELY CREATIVE NATURE IS TO STAY OUT OF YOUR OWN WAY AND LET YOURSELF BLOOM …..

The Gorpians were accustomed to working together. All were taught at a young age to see each other as flawed and ambivalent beings, each of whom was fighting their own respective inner battle. By conditioning the populace to hold up mirrors to each other's imperfections, mutual forgiveness was much more readily attained. Everyone wore yellow, green, pink and purple tie-dyed T-shirts, fabricated in the antique style of *The Grateful Dead* on the Blue Green Planet. All Gorpians were required, starting at the age of five, to study *chromesthesia*, as well as *synesthesia*, in school. Education was compulsory for all Gorpian citizens.

Planet Gorp was the ideal place to practice and perfect the arts of synesthesia and chromesthesia. Its terrain and atmosphere featured pastoral chartreuse landscapes, babbling and bubbling sky blue brooks and pale yellow skies, all of which pleasantly reverberated. The Gorpians heard colors, looked at sounds, and took deep breaths of light ….. But then one day, their state of mutual togetherness was threatened by fights that broke out over the hoarding of gorp.

Anna Thesia: EVEN THOUGH WE INHABIT A PLANET OF ABUNDANCE, THERE ARE THOSE AMONG US WHO WILL ALWAYS FALL PREY TO A BELIEF IN SCARCITY …..

As outbreaks of anger on Planet Gorp were uncommon, when anger appeared and the citizens' state of harmony turned to discord, many lifted their eyebrows in confusion, as if to say: *What? What's happening? Not cool man. Just not cool. We need to unify our vibrations and seek calm within the safety net of our collective consciousness* ….. Anna Thesia attempted to solve the gorp problem diplomatically:

Anna Thesia: (*addressing two men involved in a gorp-based conflict*) It's only gorp, it's only trail mix, my brothers. I wanted to say: IT'S ONLY FUCKING GORP! IT'S ONLY FUCKING TRAIL MIX ….. My enlightened friends. But no man, please no. No always to negative intensity, however valid it may be in terms of personal expression. No always to negative intensity, no matter how important it is in terms of truth, be it your own truth or that of your comrade. If we must swear, let us swear quietly. Let us whisper

MOTHERFUCKER gently under our collective breaths, thus transforming the brutal implication of that term into a meditative mantra. (*in a low, gentle voice*) It's all good man and the motherfuckers won't win. (*much louder*) But you know who does win? WE WIN ….. We Win ….. With peace, love and tie-dye. And when we win, it's a win-win. Do I hear a WE-WIN? Do I hear a WIN-WIN?

Gorpian Chorus: WE-WIN! WIN-WIN! WE-WIN! WIN-WIN!

Anna Thesia: MAKE YOUR SCARCITY SCARCE, BECAUSE ABUNDANCE IS ABUNDANT ….. The Universe provides, just ask the Universe for what you need and want, man. There'll always be plenty of gorp to go around because we create our own resources after visualizing what we need and want and THERE IS ENOUGH AND THERE WILL ALWAYS BE ENOUGH ….. In the cool caves that exist below the surface of our pristine world, rows upon rows of Easy Bake Ovens were installed by refugees from the Blue Green Planet. They arrived here over five hundred years ago and were the first humans to inhabit our world. And with this advanced technology, gorp can be produced forever. *GORP WILL BE PRODUCED UNTIL THE END OF TIME!* Because the Easy Bake Ovens have been rewired, upgraded and updated; that work was achieved thanks to the genius of our exceptional populace. It will serve no purpose to remind you of the dark times of hyper capitalism. No good will come from reclaiming that memory; we must never return to that era again, my enlightened friends. Here is the greatest lesson that was learned during the hyper capitalistic dark times: *Gorp is of the people, by the people, for the people.* Gorp is like stardust, it never disappears, it just takes on a new form ….. Tonight we'll build a big bonfire, a fire of ritual purification, and pray to our Cosmic Goddesses to express our gratitude for the gorp that they eternally supply to us. We will pray to the Protectors of Gorp: The High Priestess, the Empress and the Crone. NEVER FORGET THE POWER AND THE WISDOM OF OUR ELDERS. Yes, the fire illuminates, but it also makes us aware of the dark. The spirits of the night come to congregate at the periphery of the light. It's in our best interest to establish a truce with these dark spirits. We have no choice but to make friends with the night; the only way that we can overcome the darkness is to remain unafraid! For we must always live with opposites: yin yang, day and night, black and white, dark and light, sun and moon.

A woman named Eleutheria, who was known to fall into trances and hypnotic states, suddenly froze and then remained immobile as if she was possessed. The people calmly turned to observe her, as eccentrics and eccentricity were respected and praised everywhere on Planet Gorp. Eleutheria raised up her arms, threw back her head and spoke in sharp, staccato tones in a syncopated rhythm:

Eleutheria: SAY YES TO OUR GODDESS CO-PILOTESSE! SAY NO TO OUR GODDESS CO-DISTRESS! SAY YES TO OUR GODDESS CO-FINESSE! SAY YES TO OUR GODDESS CO-CARESS! ALL HAIL TO THE TRAIL MIX GODDESS! WE THANK THEE GODDESS OF TRAIL MIX!

Eleutheria starts to chant in a high, warbling vibrato.

HARMONIC CONVERGENCE! WE ARE THE RESURGENCE! COLD WATER DETERGENT! NO MORE DIVERGENCE!

Anna Thesia: You see? Sister Woman Eleutheria has the answer! She perceives and reacts to even the slightest of vibrations that emanate from the molten iron inner core of our world. There's so much we can learn from her! Think with your right brains, comrades! Don't be seduced by an addiction to the comfort provided by linear, angular, left-brain logic! Our world is round! Our world is circular! Our world is made of curves! Just like our Divine Mother Gorp!

BRYANNA DOLLS
AND CLAWDEEYA BALLS

The Birth of a Doppelgänger

When Bryanna Dolls was eleven, she gave birth to her *doppelgänger*, Clawdeeya Balls. More specifically, Clawdeeya split off from Bryanna, as a fully formed eleven year old human girl, albeit one with a completely different personality. At the age of ten, Bryanna sensed that Clawdeeya wanted to be released from within her; Clawdeeya was kicking and screaming to get out. And so Bryanna asexually produced Clawdeeya and once this birth had been achieved, both of them were greatly relieved. To have gone on as two diametrically opposed individuals, living within one body, just would have been too stressful. Bryanna Dolls stayed her good old self. The new and wicked Clawdeeya Balls became the shadow version of Bryanna …..

Bryanna Dolls had always longed to inhabit a real-life version of the film adaptation of *Valley of the Dolls*. She wished that 1967 had never ended. She dreamt of being a part of the Valley of the Dolls Triad: Neely O'Hara, Anne Wells and Jennifer North. If Bryanna had been forced to choose though, which one of the Tryppie Trynytie she could embody permanently, she would have chosen Anne Wells. This way, when times got tough, she could take the train from Nueva Jork, Puta Jork up to Connecktykoont, Northeastern Zone, Amourrica Profunda. There, she'd visit her grandmother, who lived in a gingerbread house whose grounds were carpeted with aromatic pine needles. There, grandma would be waiting to welcome Bryanna with unconditional love and freshly baked oatmeal raisin cookies. This grandmother would be the mother that she never had; a mother figure who was the exact opposite of her own ….. *Mother always reminded me, every time that I visited her, that she'd pushed me out of the nest and that she'd continue to do so for as long as she lived. And as much as I resented her for that, I was ultimately grateful. For if she'd continued to coddle and overprotect me, I would have stayed tangled in her apron strings, unwilling and unable to develop a separate and unique adult identity of my own. That being said, if only she could have raised me with a little more nurture and a little less nature …..*

In 1967, everything had been better; this was a fantasy that Bryanna had created in her mind to sustain herself through difficult times. She viewed 1967 through her rose-colored glasses, refusing to acknowledge the seriousness of the social and political upheavals of that era ..... The illegal, unwinnable war; the political polarization, the struggle for racial equality; the hippie movement that eventually unraveled and transformed itself into the decadent 1970s, as well as the crusade for women's rights and what would ultimately become the LGBTQ movement ..... There'd also been LSD, *turn on, tune in and drop out*, free love, psychedelic rock and manifestations of a cosmic consciousness, fostered by an increasing awareness of Eastern spirituality that was being incorporated into Western culture. The hippies, yippies and flower children believed that they were going to change civilization for the better, only to see their Apollonian ideals dissolve into a quagmire of Dionysian disintegration. No one in 1967 could have foreseen the backlash and the return to reactionary times that accelerated after Nine-Eleven. In 1967, there was still hope that mankind would come to its senses, stop the violence and choose instead to live in peace and harmony ..... Bryanna had not understood any of this during her 1960's childhood, but the events of that era had affected her subliminally and would end up exerting a significant influence upon her worldview. As a child, she'd wanted to grow up fast and leave her gender-neutral Barbie and Ken dolls behind her. Once she finally became an adult, she chose worldly women as role models, or rather women who were already world-weary ..... As Neely, Anne and Jennifer had been in 1967.

CLAWDEEYA BALLS
DISAPPEARS

Clawdeeya Balls had lived with her adoptive parents since she was eleven years old; she came to them under mysterious circumstances. She grew up in Drowsydayle, Orckario, Narniada. She remembered nothing of her childhood before age eleven. Mrs. Balls played the organ and was the choir director for the Drowsydayle Episcopal Church; Mr. Balls worked for the local chapter of The Disunited Dissuade. When Clawdeeya was eleven, she became popular among the neighborhood girls of her age. On warm summer evenings, they would run up to the front doorstep of the Balls' two-story 1960 Colonial, to ring the doorbell and see if Clawdeeya could come out to play. Mrs. Balls let her daughter go, but she was worried; not that the neighborhood girls would have a bad influence on Clawdeeya, but rather vice versa ..... *I know that times have changed*, Mrs. Balls thought to herself ..... *But there's something about Clawdeeya that's just too aggressive, and too forward thinking, for any girl of any time* ….. When she was twelve years old, Clawdeeya went through puberty. Compared to other girls her age, she didn't experience any noticeable shame, insecurity or denial. She appeared to be handling her budding sexuality with confidence. By the time she was fourteen, she was known to be sexually precocious. By the time Clawdeeya was fifteen, she'd become a joker, trickster and troublemaker. From that time on, her social life became something of a mystery, but she still managed to get good grades in all of her high school courses. At age sixteen, she started thinking about her future and researching colleges; she was planning her escape. At seventeen, she began submitting applications to various institutions of higher learning, mainly to schools that were as far away from her parents as possible.

….. One evening, Mrs. Balls was woken up by her awareness of a pulsating, white luminescence that was shining through the front window of the second floor master bedroom like a floodlight. She jumped up in alarm and yanked back the diaphanous, pale blue curtains. A cylindrical beam of radiant white light, nine feet in diameter, rose up into the sky and thereafter out of sight. It was emanating from below their front yard, just beyond the two crab-apple trees that stood on the north side of the driveway. And caught within this beam ….. suspended ….. levitating ….. was Clawdeeya. She was floating and not fully conscious. Perhaps she was in a trance; maybe a spell had been cast upon her and she was dreaming. Suddenly her shoulders slumped, her head began to loll around, her eyeballs rolled up behind her eyelids and she started to shake. The beam of light that entrapped Clawdeeya began to vibrate and then reverberate, as if the light were also sound. She started muttering, her eyes opened wide; she looked confused and terrified. The intensity of the light's vibrations increased. She was being pulled up and down by an unknown force. Successive claps of thunder were heard and then lightning struck the two crabapple trees, splitting both of their trunks in half. And then all at once, in the midst of this chaos, Clawdeeya and the luminous beam vanished.

Mrs. Balls closed the curtains, folded her arms and sighed. She exited the bedroom to go downstairs. Her husband was still asleep; he could sleep through anything. She made her way to the kitchen that featured beige walls, black and white linoleum flooring, sepia cupboards and reddish-brown, wooden window blinds with maneuverable slats. A sea foam green Formica table stood next to a bay window; the bay window looked out onto a ravine that sloped downwards towards a creek. The four chairs that accompanied the Formica table were embellished with shiny sea foam green padded coverings ….. Mrs. Balls opened the doors of the liquor cabinet above the refrigerator. She took out a bottle of cognac, got a tumbler out of the kitchen cupboard and poured the cognac into the tumbler (everyone else who lived in her neighborhood would have referred to the cognac as brandy, but not Mrs. Balls because she was classy). As she sipped on her drink, she thought to herself ….. *Well isn't it a shame that Clawdeeya's gone, but then again, now she won't have to attend college. I'm not so sure she was suited for an academic education in the first place. Not everyone needs to go to college to make something of themselves in this life. I always thought she'd be better off working with her hands. I hope she's happy wherever she's ended up ….. Could she have been abducted by aliens?* But Mrs. Balls' ruminating amounted to nothing more than a rationalization of her true feelings towards Clawdeeya. She couldn't relate to Clawdeeya and so she wasn't sure whether she cared about this girl, who six years earlier had first appeared to Mrs. Balls and her husband. She knew that she wasn't going to lose any sleep over Clawdeeya's disappearance, at least not that evening. Clawdeeya had always been a handful and more trouble than she'd been worth.

The next morning, Mrs. Balls opened the front door to retrieve the morning paper. A letter, consisting of black crayon scrawled on sheets of crinkled white notebook paper, was lying on the front doorstep. It read as follows:

Dear Amazing, Wonderful, Precious Mother (Just kidding! I hate you, you fucked up, alcoholic, suburban, valium-inhaling trophy wife! I curse the day that you were born!). But seriously, Mother: you know that I always had an edgy sense of humor. Just wanted to let you know that I've gone on an epic journey to the planet Alphagamoria, where I've secured an internship in a space kickboxing program. Once I've finished that apprenticeship, I will make my professional debut in a contest that will take place in the Galatea galaxy. There, I will challenge my nemesis, alter ego and doppelgänger Bryanna Dolls. I'm gonna kick ass and send prissy Bryanna Dolls up into the stratosphere. Dude! She won't even know what hit her! Ten seconds after the referee starts the match, she'll be rocketing up and out into deep space. Don't wait up; I won't be back for a couple of years. Even though I'll be making my

return journey at the speed of light …..
Alphagamoria is very, very far away!

With vile, visceral and venomous hatred,

Your Steampunk-Fiend-Zombie-
Vampire-Werewolf Daughter,

Clawdeeya Balls, also known as The
Queen of Black Holes and Intergalactic
Dark Matter

PS – Hey Frienemy! If you start to miss
me, light some candles late at night on
the kitchen table while Daddy's sleep-
ing (and while you're drinking, you fuck-
ing drunk!). Ha ha, you know that I'm
kidding; I always liked to hit the bottle
too whenever you and Daddy would
take off on the weekends for your
bird watching trips. But seriously: light
seven candles and pray to Bastet, the
Egyptian Cat Goddess. The modern
day domestic housecat, Felis silvestris
lybica, originated in North Africa. We
owe the ancient Egyptian culture our
undying respect! Don't say that I never
did you any favors!

After reading the note from her daughter, Mrs.
Balls stared at a decorative jade green ceramic

ashtray in the center of the kitchen table. She got up from the table, looked inside the cupboard above the stove and pulled out a box of kitchen matches. She proceeded to light a match and burn the let-ter from Clawdeeya as she prayed to Bastet, as her daughter had advised …..

BASTET THE EGYPTIAN CAT GODDESS

And what she had written was a convoluted yet confessional, erratic yet elucidating analysis. Henceforth, there would be no more sophomoric simplifications. She made it her life's work to remind us, that though our truths may differ and although we may not find common ground in our discussions of the harsh realities of existence ….. Nevertheless, a mutual respect for the gravitas inspired by those subjects of significance, upon which certain enlightened beings choose to ruminate and pontificate, shall remain in effect as *We the People* gather united under the rubric of *Joseph's Coat of Many Colored Rainbow Flags*, those being comprised of an infinite number of gradations within gradations originating in a heretofore unknown and kaleidoscopically spectral multiverse ….. And regarding whichever way the not-so-fine-upstanding citizens of Amourrica Profunda choose to exercise their insidious, clandestine and yet mutually agreed upon perverse and personal practices ….. As long as no one is injured or violated in the process, none of the alleged instigators shall be pestered, pursued or persecuted. The time for puritanical witch hunts has come and gone; outdated superstitions such at these became irrelevant after the arrival of the Age of Illumination ….. And though the petty squabbles of a polarized populace may multiply in the Land of the Quasi-Pseudo-Free, the aforementioned conflicts shall be resolved with maternal empathy and compassion by Bastet, also known as *The One-Eyed Pyramid Goddess* (she who was previously celebrated as *The All-Seeing Eye of Providence*). Bastet is endowed with many faces and she wears a lot of hats. Her alternate identities are as follows: Kali-Shiva, Creator-Destroyer; *Brünnhilde, Wagnerian heroine-martyr* and Maleficent, sorceress and potentate of evil incarnate ….. Bastet possesses the wisdom of the Violet Seventh Chakra and the power of the One Ring that must be cast back into the fiery chasm from whence it came. And though what is spoken here may sound grandiloquent to uninformed ears, don't be fooled, *The One-Eyed Pyramid Goddess*, despite her impressive powers, can be silly when it suits her. She's not above making an off-color joke or delving into *risqué* humor, although her contradictory nature may inspire her at any instant to retreat into the cloister of her cloudy purple-black moods ….. For Bastet was a troubled adolescent once, who kept a diary in which she made scribblings of hearts, flowers, suns, moons and stars, that accompanied poetry ….. Of the kind lacking an awareness of mortality that can only be found among the young, who still believe that they will live forever. Within her diary, archetypal symbols were used to create her own special alphabet, in case that diary would end up being preserved and then found by advanced extraterrestrial civilizations in the future ….. Bastet treads silently across the savannah. She lounges in trees, swats her tail and relaxes in the underbrush where she remains camouflaged. She walks behind you and you are unaware of her presence. She pinpoints her potential victims, hidden from view, obscured in the background. She bides her time, until it's too late and her prey has been captured and devoured. Bastet will never be tamed; she will always exist in the purgatory between the beauty and horror of the natural and supernatural worlds. *At night all cats are gray* …..

CLAWDEEYA BALLS TAKES ON THE WORLD

After having split apart from Bryanna Dolls, Clawdeeya Balls grew up to be a complete and utter monster, who foisted herself upon the human race with bravado, panache and chutzpah. Clawdeeya was nineteen now and she'd decided that college was bullshit. Instead, she focused on being a manic, aggressive, self-destructive witch who lived by a code of ongoing *Schadenfreude*. Men, as well as women, were attracted to her animal sexuality. But most of them ended up ignoring her for the other twenty-three and one half hours of the day. Which is not to say that she found it easy to get lucky; she was the opposite of approachable. In fact, the only thing that kept Clawdeeya out of jail was her knowledge of black magic, which she'd learned from watching 1970s *ABC TV Movies of the Week* ..... Clawdeeya was ambitious; she knew what she wanted and she knew how she was going to get it. After an eighteen-month internship in a space kickboxing program on the planet Alphagamoria in the Androgynous galaxy, she'd returned to the Blue Green Planet with a renewed sense of purpose. As she walked by the businessmen of downtown Near-Wanna, Orckario, Narniada, as they left their offices in the late afternoon, she was brewing with hatred. On any other day, she would have told any one of them to fuck off, in an explicit way that they wouldn't soon forget. Instead, she chose to stay calm so as not to cloud her mind with anger. She needed clarity in that moment to help her focus on the preparation of her nefarious plans ….. To let off some steam, she'd developed an alter ego. She was moonlighting as a standup comic, who wrote her own material and played around at the local clubs. She dressed in a style that she used to intimidate the crowd. Her look was Goth and she decked herself out in the witchy attire of that genre: white face makeup, black lip-stick, black eyebrows, eyebrow ring, nose ring, black long-sleeved dresses and black boots with black laces. For that evening, she'd secured a 10 pm spot at Harry's House of Hacks …..

Male Emcee: Hey everybody! How's it goin'? How you doin'? Our next comedian to grace the stage is a disturbing young woman who goes by the name of ….. Well, I'll just bring her up! Laidies and gentleman of whatever persuasion, orientation, denomination or classification ….. Including those of you who don't want to be embarrassed in public, but who most likely will be by our next performer ….. PLEASE WELCOME ….. CLAWDEEYA BALLS …..

The audience applauds politely.

Clawdeeya Balls (*with intense sarcasm*): WOW! It's such a coincidence, that here I am going on at Harry's House of Hacks. Because before I came here tonight, I was thinking about how long it's been since I'd had the opportunity to torture a delightful audience like yourselves, with one of the hackiest of hack standup routines ever created, which happens to be my specialty. On that note, I shall proceed ….. ANYONE SINGLE? ANYONE DATING? ANYONE IN THERAPY? ANYONE MASTURBATING? PLEASE STOP MASTURBATING IN PUBLIC! YOU'RE DISGUSTING! ANYONE ON OPIOIDS? ANYONE BANKRUPT BECAUSE YOU COULDN'T AFFORD TO BUY HEALTH INSURANCE? And before I get to my A-List material, here's a reminder: CAREFUL! WATCH OUT! WITH A MERE SWIVEL OF MY HIPS, I'LL ANNIHILATE YOU WITH MY NEWLY ACQUIRED BOTOX BUBBLEBUTT!….. Just kidding. FEEL FREE TO TALK AMONGST YOURSELVES AND TRASH MY FAT ASS! But seriously, *mesdames et messieurs*: ARE ANY OF THE MEN IN ATTENDANCE FETISHISTIC PERVERTS WHO BLACKMAIL WOMEN INTO PARTICIPATING IN WARPED, EXTRACURRICULAR SCENES? DO ANY OF YOU SO-CALLED GENTLEMEN

HAPPEN TO BE SEXUALLY HARASSING, SEXUALLY ASSAULTING RAPISTS? IF I FIND OUT THAT YOU ARE ….. OH MY GODDESS! YOU WILL BE SO OFF-WORLD, MAN BITCHES …..

Fifteen minutes later, as Clawdeeya Balls ended her set, the spectators remained in stunned and shocked silence, not knowing what they'd witnessed; not having understood a word of what they'd heard. During the next act, the emcee took Clawdeeya aside, advising her to work on her act, get more experience and try to modulate her persona, to make it more appealing to a typical comedy club audience. Clawdeeya listened to the emcee's advice in a state of minimal tolerance. Once he'd finished with her, she replied to him, pulling no punches: I'LL DO WHATEVER THE FUCK I WANT. I HAVE A WHOLE OTHER GIGANTIC CAREER THAT I'M FAILING AT. POINT BEING: IT'S ALL RELATIVE. HAVE A LOVELY EVENING, SIR. And with that, she left the club in a huff …..

THE METAMORPHOSIS OF MERCURY CREEK

Clawdeeya Balls' vengeance knew no bounds when indulging in the practice of maliciously joyful acts. She'd end up converting the province of Orckario into one of the most hellish destinations on the Blue Green Planet ….. Her first target was a resort, about two hours north of Near-Wanna, called Mercury

Creek. The preferred sport of Mercury Creek's clientele was golf, a sport that Clawdeeya had always despised for the way that it represented the stifling conventions of wealthy, privileged and entitled men. The grounds of Mercury Creek were covered with a layer of Monsanto green grass (*Monsanto green* very closely resembles *Day-Glo* or *fluorescent green*). This grass obscured a narrow layer of topsoil that barely concealed a massive concentration of toxic black sludge ….. Clawdeeya reached the place in the late afternoon, flying in on her Antagonystyck 7000, a broom bequeathed to her by Antithesis Reticence, Headmaster of the Szczmawgwhorets Ackademie of Sorcerie. She arrived disguised in a pale yellow tennis outfit, so that the management wouldn't suspect that she was up to something untoward. She paid for a room in the complex in which she'd spend the night. The next day, on Narniada Day (a national holiday) she waited in the partly cloudy sky, hovering in the pilot's seat of her Anti-Wonder Woman Invisibull Plane (one of several modes of transportation that she had at her disposal) waiting to wreak havoc upon the preppy patrons of Mercury Creek. A sizable group, comprised mostly of men, was golfing that day. They were dressed in pink alligator shirts, kelly green khakis, navy blue whale-embroidered belts and horrifically tacky white leather shoes with tassels. Clawdeeya wasted no time in getting to work.

….. All at once, thirty-six foot high walls of six foot thick Plexiglas rose up from the ground, to form a square that surrounded the entire eighteen-hole golf course. Dense gray-purple clouds formed over the resort, blocking out the hazy sunshine. Everyone on the course looked up, alert and concerned ….. Was Narniada being attacked by Isolamicka, its cruel and ignorant neighbor to the south? Had Isolamicka's buffoon of a leader, Turmerico Inflammatorio, initiated the sequence that would unleash irreversible nukeyuhlur devastation from which the Blue Green Planet would never recover? These were dark geopolitical times and one never knew what kind of crisis would arise on any given day ….. Dense black golf balls began to fall from the sky like mini-meteors, quickly filling up the course within its Plexiglas enclosure. The players were hit and felled and all of them died instantly. Then tremendous heat and pressure, equivalent to one billion years of sustained geological processes, were applied within the Plexiglas box, smashing down everything contained within it. All of the deceased were converted into diamonds, which made them so much more valuable dead than alive ….. Then all became silent, the gray-purple clouds cleared away and nothing could be heard in this otherwise isolated region ….. But birds chirping, bubbling brooks babbling and the call of loons traversing nearby lakes.

For a brief moment Clawdeeya Balls felt calm and serene; maybe she didn't need to instigate any more apocalyptic drama going forward. Then again, there were just too many fucked up men on the planet and even seeing a few of them undergo *transformation* gave her such a sense of relief. Not that she particularly cared for her own sex, but at least she could identify with women. She felt so good about what she'd achieved that she considered checking into a local bed and breakfast, to relax in a cozy attic studio with a skylight and while away some time crocheting a pink and blue baby shawl. But then the urge welled up within her, as she stood on top of her Anti-Wonder Woman Invisibull Plane, to finish the job that had not yet been completed to her satisfaction ..... *Phosphorescent purple jets of flame flew out of Clawdeeya's smoky black eyes, creating a mile wide crater that encompassed the resort. All of the animate and inanimate matter that had been converted into sparkling diamonds tumbled into the crater that was now hurling up lava from its depths. That Which Was Formerly Known As Mercury Creek was then dissolved within an exploding caldera that was directly connected to the molten iron inner core of the Blue Green Planet .....*

Despite her stunning accomplishment, Clawdeeya decided not to take a break; there was so much that remained to be done. First of all, she prayed to her spirit guides, that being her latest Unholie Trynytie: (1) Baba Yaga, the Retro Throwback Goddess; (2) Bastet, the Egyptian Cat Goddess; and (3) the No-Nonsense Women of the Psychobilly Culture of Branighan, Missoolah, Isolamicka ….. After this, she'd metamorphose into the form of Bobby Chooshingoorah and use his appropriated identity to control his courtesan-concubine Isabella Gloucester. As Clawdeeya felt threatened by women like Isabella, extreme action had to be taken. She would do whatever it took to ensure that no woman ever challenged her power …..

Clawdeeya: (*gleefully*) Oh my Pantheon of Goddesses! That Isabella Gloucester! She just thinks she's so good and appropriate. Who died and left her boss? So she's a Girl Scout trapped in the body of an adult female? No way! I can't wait to slut shame her; I wanna slut shame her right now! Because there's nothing worse than the hypocrisy of a floozy who acts like she's Mother Teresa ….. And the moral of this story is: SLUT + HUSH MONEY = SLUSH FUND!

DYASPORA NEOSPORYN

Bryanna Dolls never wanted to be the good girl. But she knew that she didn't want to be Clawdeeya Balls. Bryanna had never been competitive and she had no need to prove to anyone that she was the so-called best. She saw no value in having to prove that she was right or that she had to be the winner. She didn't associate being passive with either losing or being the victim. And just because she could play the gun moll or the femme fatale, didn't mean that she was going to be taking any shit from some suave crazy gangster who tried to keep her holed up in a flea bag hotel in downtown Lost Angelist ….. Thus when she told her man that she was just stepping out for a moment to get some smokes, she had no time to lose. It was time for her getaway, she only needed a few things, she could pack in a flash. He was in the shower, so he had no idea that she was carrying a suitcase ….. Then she was out on the street and cutting her way down a secluded alley to keep out of sight; it was a miracle that she'd gotten out of there in time. But the passageway she'd taken kept getting darker and darker until suddenly, while stretching out her hands in front of her in the pitch black darkness, she was tumbling, falling ..... Down, down, down she fell, though she felt like she was floating ..... The darkness didn't let up for about five minutes and then she finally saw what appeared to be a door opening beneath her, from which light, music and the noise of a crowd were emanating .....

..... She walked in through the door, unnoticed by the swarm of people that she encountered. Even though she was a looker, she'd learned how to make herself invisible. It was a survival skill; in her rush to escape, there'd been no time for makeup anyways ..... A psychedelic blues band with a raw-voiced female lead vocal, circa 1967, was playing. The band was decked out in the attire of that time; maroon paisley and purple crushed velvet; bohemian, whimsical and flamboyant. In contrast to their Haight-Ashburyesque appearance, the backup singers and dancers were wholesome, TV-friendly girls with white headbands, sleeveless white blouses, pleated white skirts and white patent leather go-go boots. They looked like Richard Nixon's cheerleaders. They danced the Twist, the Swim, the Monkey, the Mashed Potato and the Watusi. There were giant lava lamps on either side of the stage and an Electric

Kool-Aid Acid Test light show playing on a screen behind the proscenium. For Bryanna, this was like a trip back to her childhood that she was now able to experience as an adult. But before she even had a chance to start enjoying herself, the lights began to dim and the music was fading out ….. Something was pulling Bryanna to her right; she found herself in a somber corner and turned around, facing what moments ago had been the audience. She was standing stage left. All of the color had been sucked out of the room; it was now gray and eerie. Looking out into the darkness, she saw three Eurasian witches, who were lean but strong. Bryanna was back in her *noir* world, that was her natural element …..

….. The Eurasian witches had long gray-white-black hair that was knotty, ragged and unkempt. They were dressed in ash colored, sackcloth robes. White makeup, with a hint of light blue, had been applied to their faces, necks, feet and hands. A cauldron simmered in front of them as they chatted quietly. Then they began to laugh; their laughter became louder and louder. They started to stare at Bryanna and point at her while continuing with their cackling. Bryanna turned around and noticed that another small door had opened behind her, but this time the light inside was dim and ominous. As she backed away from the witches and towards the forbidding portal, the middle witch lifted up her arms and began shrieking in a Central Asian language. Then two strong cold hands grabbed Bryanna by the ankles, though she never hit the floor; her body was suspended a few inches above the ground. She was being pulled through the murky gray entranceway. Once inside, the door slammed shut and she heard a woman's stern voice say to her ..... *From now on, you will be known as Dyaspora Neosporyn. For the time being Bryanna Dolls will exist in a state of suspended animation. More will be revealed to you, but you're not ready for that yet. To prepare you for your metamorphosis, you will go into a trance* ..... And with that, Bryanna Dolls, now Dyaspora Neosporyn, fell into a dream .....

..... The grave consequences of global warming had arrived. She was trudging through a lush jungle that had sprung up over what used to be tundra. Giant mosquitoes were flying along beside her; they carried Zeema and other diseases. They were hunting down potential human victims, to suck their blood and make them ill. Dyaspora was trying to swat them to death with two tennis rackets, one in each hand. But it was hopeless, there were just too many of them. She wasn't worried about the high carbon dioxide levels, her gas mask had been securely fitted over her face ..... Then she found herself in a place where anarchic scientists had taken to recycling materials leftover from the discarded remnants

of the antiquated infrastructure of the latest plutocratic regime (whose subjects had been reduced to
scrambling for the few remaining resources). Glass
tunnels connected a succession of hothouses that
had been constructed to replace outmoded agri-
cultural methods ….. Dyaspora watched people fall
into sinkholes leading to methane springs that had
been created by the melting of the permafrost.
*Life has always been a gamble, no risk no reward,
extreme planet equals extreme adventure, opportunity awaits those who are willing to look at the glass
half full* ….. She walked on and suddenly she was
standing in a check-in line at an airport. She'd spon-
taneously decided to buy a ticket to somewhere,
just for the hell of it. Who said you had to stop traveling just because the climate had gone haywire? She
wasn't worried about the severe turbulence as she
flew over Mount Doom on Kompot Airlines, on the
way to the Ring of Fire that bordered the Western
Ocean. The plane was flying upside down, but she
was securely strapped into her seat and felt completely relaxed. She was watching *Mad Men* on a TV
screen embedded into the back of the seat ahead
of her and thanking her Cosmic Goddesses that
she'd escaped from that mosquito-laden jungle …..

….. Then Dyaspora Neosporyn found herself in
the upstairs bedroom of a Southern mansion. She
was lying under pale yellow sheets and a beige

chenille bedspread. As she woke up, everything was blurry, but within five minutes her vision had cleared. A woman with ashy blonde hair, coiffed in an early 1960's style, was pacing back and forth. Her arms were folded and she was smoking a cigarette. She was wearing a string of pearls, a sleeveless gold blouse, a light olive skirt and champagne high heels. Dyaspora followed this female with her eyes until finally the woman caught her glance. She walked over and started to address Dyaspora in her Southern accent ….. *Hello honey child well look at you and aren't we happy to have you back in the land of the living! You've had quite a journey from the looks of it and we don't know where you came from, but don't you worry, we'll redefine whatever notion you had of the word "hospitality". We'll get you all fixed up, back up on your feet and indoctrinated in no time. By the way, I'm Ophelia; Ophelia Wainwright! Pleased as punch to meet you* …… As Dyaspora had no idea what she was going to be indoctrinated into, she immediately felt a tinge of fear. She tried to pull herself up but the effort exhausted her. Eventually, she made it to a sitting position and managed to prop up a pillow behind her back ….. *That's right sugar now you get comfortable* ….. *You're going to need to get your strength back before your orientation* ….. (with humor yet vaguely threatening) *We run a tight ship down here, no fooling around, oh yes you're going to be learning a thing or two, you'll see and you'll be so glad that you did* ….. Dyaspora decided that she should proceed by presenting herself as normally as possible, and in so doing, study this woman who seemed to be holding her hostage, although not forcibly. She would find out who this female was and what she wanted. She began to feel afraid again ….. What if she had no power here? Who the hell was Ophelia Wainwright and where the hell were they? The bedroom reminded her of Brick and Maggie's bedroom in *Cat On A Hot Tin Roof*. But before Dyaspora could summon up the nerve to say something, Ophelia started speaking to her again.

Ophelia: I can read your mind, Miss Neosporyn, and to answer your question: you're in Bitoxia, a subtropical town in the state of Archaicka in the Confederate Region of Isolamicka. And I'm going to tell you all about it, whether you like it or not ….. I'll never forget the day that Daddy died; the Spanish moss was swaying gently in the sweltering breeze. My feelings towards him had always been ambivalent. We'd never been close; children were to be seen and not heard! We never enjoyed that special bond that fathers and daughters often have. Which is not to say that I was close to my mother either; I could never get a word in edgewise with her. To say that she was a character would be the understatement of the year! You couldn't find a more compelling antagonist if you were to comb through every

Greek tragedy ever written ..... One night shortly after Daddy's funeral, I was swept up in a feverish dream and I found myself face to face with my dearly departed father's presence. He shimmered before me like Hamlet's ghost ..... Why was I seeing this and where had he come from? After having experienced this disturbing vision, I took to my majestic canopy bed that was covered with mosquito netting, still devastated. Would this grief ever pass? God knows that I needed distraction, so I fanned myself wistfully and imagined myself being courted by a bevy of gentleman callers, all of whom were blessed with an advanced socioeconomic stature ..... I know what you're thinking, Miss Dyaspora; that everything's segregated down here. So let's get right to the heart of the matter, shall we? That which is forbidden, in other words the taboo of interracial love, has generated so much excitement throughout our Confederate history. My cultural conditioning won't allow me to speak about it though, because if I were to expose that subject to the light of day, it would lose all of its seductive power. And I'd rather tantalize you with the mystery of that which remains unexpressed .....

..... I've always been spoiled; I'll admit that. As a child, I was given anything that money could buy. But I've never taken it for granted. Daddy used to be in the import-export business and he always said that

I was gifted with a baroque sensibility. He believed that I had a future in the appraisal of florid tapestries, ornate wall hangings and scintillating carpets originating in those cities that were linked by the Silk Road. But I had no desire to travel; it was enough for me to tour Europa for that year between high school and college and then for another year again after graduating from Tulane University, where I was a liberal arts major. My friend Sebastian used to kiddingly call Europa *"Boyropa"* ..... Child! Honey! Sugar! I was absolutely scandalized to discover that he had an interest in the boys of which I was previously unaware ..... I never felt European; I felt no connection with European ways. I tried to learn foreign languages, but putting them into practice was simply beyond my capability. What influence could I ever have as an importer-exporter? It would have all been so draining, having to play the role of a sophisticated woman, to court favor with my colleagues and competitors. I am in no way cosmopolitan and never wanted to be. I am a child at heart, and an evil one mind you, like one of those demonic children from *The Village of the Damned* .....

..... Our stunning, magnificent Christmas tree, which goes up without fail the day after Thanksgiving, is crowded with ornaments made in Cathay, by a people who have no appreciation for monotheism (or Evilangelism as we practice it down here).

Although for a country whose citizens think of themselves as Communists, they sure have a well-developed understanding of capitalism. I never earned the right to discuss the world at large and it made no difference, I was never going to leave this mansion .....
As a child, I was psychologically harassed, terrorized and traumatized by every one of my family members and by every man I ever knew. I'd set goals for myself, which I had every intention of achieving, but whenever I tried to turn those dreams into reality, all I got was pushback from a world that kept telling me: *NO NO NO, YOU CAN'T DO THAT, WE DON'T WANT YOU, WE DON'T NEED YOU, WE'RE NOT INTERESTED IN YOU!* Even my closest friends, who I sought out for advice, gave me no encouragement whatsoever regarding the pursuit of my aspirations, making something of myself and becoming the person that I was meant to be. I should have trusted myself; I should have listened to those inner voices that encouraged me. But I gave in to the negative voices, I stopped trying; what did it matter? I knew that I'd always be able to live in comfort and security; I'd never end up on the street or God forbid homeless ..... Barring a conscious decision to hurl myself into a downward spiral or the occurrence of some unforeseen apocalyptic catastrophe. As a result of everything I've described, I decided to retreat from the world into this, my cloister; I got me to my nunnery .....

….. Dyaspora was drifting back to sleep. This Ophelia and her privilege-based battle that she was fighting within had become so draining that Dyaspora had to block it out by returning to her slumber ….. When she woke up again, she was in a completely different world. She opened her eyes and saw nothing but blackness; it was night plus night squared. Gradually, her surroundings came into focus ….. First everything was a hazy indigo and then a grayish blue. Dyaspora was sitting on a bed, on top of black sheets and a black bedspread, with her back against a silver pillow. She was wearing a little girl's white dress in the style of Shirley Temple. She was in a gloomy chamber that resembled an underground prison cell. Ophelia Wainwright was no longer there. Another woman had taken her place: a tough looking, glamorous, Gothic empress. She was wearing pale white makeup with black eyebrows, black eyeliner, thick black mascara and black lipstick. She looked like Maleficent. The expression on her face was chilling; her voice was deep and powerful. She smiled in a way that in any other context would have been comical ….. *Hello* ….. she enunciated slowly ….. *Bryanna Dolls, I presume? I am Luchadora Madrugadora, Queen of Stepford Ken And Barbie Westworld. (flippantly) And just because I like to sleep late, doesn't mean that I'm lazy ….. Your indoctrination will be starting very soon and then you will be porn-key teleported off world. I hope you are ready. I hope you are prepared. Listen well. Click your white patent leather heels together three times and then chant the name of your doppelgänger obsessively: CLAWDEEYA BALLS ….. CLAWDEEYA BALLS ….. CLAWDEEYA BALLS ….. The time for your reunion with Clawdeeya Balls has arrived …..*

….. Luchadora began to cackle wickedly, her laughter becoming louder and louder as it echoed throughout the chamber. Bryanna Dolls clicked her white patent leather heels together three times. She was terrified, but felt a tremendous surge of relief once her porn-key teleportation had commenced…..

THE ULTIMATE CONTEST

TOMMY MASSAGENY

It was a boxing ring suspended in space in the heart of the Galatea galaxy. It was enclosed within a bubble that contained a breathable atmosphere. This is where the contestants would fight their respective battles. Each of them would arrive from their particular corner of the Universe; from their planets, star systems and vast expanses of dark matter that rendered cloaking devices obsolete. Each of them would make an entrance in their silver space chariots. And none other than Tommy Massageny would referee the fight. He'd come a long way since his troubled childhood in Bitoxia, Archaicka, Confederate Region, Isolamicka, Blue Green Planet. There, he'd grown up in a trailer with his parents, behind the mansion owned by the family of Ophelia Wainwright. There was so much he'd gotten over, let go of and left behind. Yes, there'd been damage, but Tommy had no time for baggage, resentments or mulling over the past. He was forward thinking to the extreme, as this was the only way he could survive. Tommy was a fighter and there was nothing in Beelzebub's unblessed inferno that was going to stop him from getting what he wanted ….. How, when and where he wanted it. Tommy was gifted with the power of artifice. He could cut through the boring and the mundane with his exceptional ability to fiercely sugarcoat the essence of any situation. Artifice, as he practiced and presented it, was not only an attribute and a strength; it was also a weapon …..

Tommy Massageny was supremely attired for the occasion; his current wardrobe redefined flamboyant. As he stood in the boxing ring getting psyched for the big event to start, the spectators who'd arrived early admired his outfit. His ensemble combined late phase 1970s Elvis Presley and mid-1970s androgynous glitter glam rock. It also incorporated punk, post punk, new wave and new romantic elements from the late 1970s and early 1980s. And despite associations that would be made with breeder styles, the way Tommy wore his costume, and his manner of working it as he wore it, was so outlandishly gay that even the haters and homophobes admired and respected his outrageous choice of couture. Whenever Tommy entered any room, it was as if the closet door had swung wide open and the space was illuminated by a floodlight that exposed and banished every secret and skeleton that happened to be lurking in any obscure corners. The only way that his outfit deferred to the current, politically correct and mainstream-leaning aspect of LGBTQ culture was this: It was a rainbow suit. But it was a rainbow suit that reconceived the symbol by eclipsing the dull, bland and pastel LGBTQ rainbow flag, to which various subgroups and subcultures of the LGBTQ demographic pledged no allegiance whatsoever. It was a form-fitting body suit; a costume that only a man under forty years of age could wear without being ridiculed. And let's not forget the accessories: rainbow cowboy hat, oversized rainbow sunglasses, rainbow evening gloves, rainbow cowboy boots and an extra large rainbow umbrella. His platinum blonde hairstyle could be described as *Flock of Seagulls meets Marie Antoinette*. All of the fabric of his costume, that was made of vegetable-based plastic, was uniformly covered with one inch wide, alternating vertical stripes of neon yellow, Day-Glo pink and iridescent sky blue. The hues were so vibrant, that the spectators in attendance were required to wear specially designed protective sunglasses to prevent them from being blinded by the brilliance of Tommy's outfit.

The spectators had shown up on their various, elaborate deep space vehicles, which valet parking took care of for the duration of the event. Once they'd gone through the decompression chambers and then security, the barcodes on their tickets were unlocked, by means of creative visualization, and their reserved seats materialized instantly. They then took their places on all four sides of the boxing ring ..... The tournament was about to begin. Tommy relished the attention that he was receiving from the crowd as he awaited the arrival of the competitors. He signaled the audience by waving his arms over his head, before making the following announcement:

Tommy Massageny: (*high energy*) I just want y'all to know that I think you're truly special, and that even if you don't feel special at this particular moment, bitch please get it together, don't even think about workin' my last nerve while I'm workin' my runway honey! Just fake it till you make it and pretend you're special and no attitude! This is an attitude free zone, attitude *verboten!* Or will mama have to turn into the freakin' *fascista?* Attitude free, at least until the end of this event! How about we keep it shallow and silly tonight, because life's too short and there's so many questions that will just never be answered! You got problems Grrrl? Go read a self-help book and learn how to think positively! Make peace with your demons or at least channel them into something sparkling! SPARKLE, NEELY, SPARKLE! That's my preferred modus operandi and if I can do it, so can you! As long as we wear our masks of *joie de vivre* twenty-four seven, we can make like it's Carnival every day! Ain't no one gonna bring me down tonight OR EVUH! YAAAAAS KWEEEEN ….. And don't let anyone objectify you, unless you want to be objectified yourself! *Mkay?* Objectification only by mutual consent! Yes men are pigs, but let us never forget to practice mutual consent between pigs ….. I wish I could call this the Gay Space Games, but the participants of this event have not been confirmed as having come out of the closet, even though as we all know, everyone in the cosmos is gay. And there's no way I'll be calling it the LGBTQ Space Games because LGBTQ as a moniker is just so tired, peer pressure and follow the herd; I didn't invent it! Most importantly, I can't call it the Gay Space Games because it's only a one-night stand, Grrrl! You want categories? I'll give you this then: *THIS IS NOT A HETERONORMATIVE EVENT! AND IT'S NOT A HOMONORMATIVE EVENT EITHER! IT'S AN OMNINORMATIVE EVENT!* Isn't it fabulous that we live in an era in which not only our genders and sexuality are mutable, but also one in which time can be bent, shaped, twisted, reversed and accelerated? ….. When I was a teenager in Bitoxia, Archaicka, the local numerologist told me this: If you plan on getting anywhere in life, you'd better get in touch with your feminine side, Grrrl! So please follow my advice and do that presto pronto right the fuck now! The Universe will thank you and reward you with a lifetime's supply of good karma! Honey, when I start runnin' my mouth, I just can't stop! Bear with me, one last thing: our theme for tonight is the following: *Hashtag Yay!* Make like its Hashtag Yay! But in the interest of keeping things real, let's all chant Men Are Pigs as well! *Hashtag Men Are Pigs!* Repeat after me: YAY YAY YAY! MEN ARE PIGS! Is everybody having a good time? I can't hear you! You'll have to do better than that for Mama! IS EVERYBODY HAVING A GOOD TIME?

The crowd responds with whoops and hollers of approval.

Spectators (*chanting*): YAY YAY YAY! MEN ARE PIGS! YAY YAY YAY! MEN ARE PIGS …..

Tommy Massageny: Okay, you've got the spirit! Here we go! Laidies and gentleman of every persuasion, be it heterosexual, homosexual, sexually ambiguous, sexually amphibious, asexual, ambivalent, intersex, indeterminate, post-gender, transgender, transcender, transsexual, transvestite, or hermaphrodite (don't worry, I'm not forgetting about all the rest of you who just go about your business and don't give a flyin' fuck about no labels) ….. Listen closely, because what I'm going to say is deep, child: We are gathered here for a fight that will not only determine the fate of the participants, but may very well change the destinies of every one of us! Any minute now, Luchadora Madrugadora, Bryanna Dolls, Ophelia Wainwright and Clawdeeya Balls will be flying in from their points of origin. This will be a contest for the ages! *Grrrl You Know It's True!* Okay let's get this party started!

The Intergalactic Institute's Inspirational Band of Badass Bitches, Cultivated Queens, Curious Queers, Unscrupulous Screamers, Pansexual Pansies, Naughty Nenas, Nerve-Wracking Nellies, Fabulous Fag Hags and Sweet Transvestites starts to play. The music has been created with the exact specifications of the diva-worshipping crowd in mind. Just as the audience is starting to get lost in the music, the band stops abruptly and vrooming noises of sonic proportions are heard in the distance.

Tommy: Our contestants are approaching! May the best woman win! No one fucks with these women! Once the winner has been confirmed and the stardust has settled, multidirectional, positive vibrations will be traveling at the speed of light to every corner of the Universe ….. That's just a small part of a series of multiverses that we can't even begin to imagine! In closing, let me say this: THIS WILL BE A WIN WIN, IT'S ALL GOOD, WE GOT THIS, JUST DO IT….. LET'S DO THIS ….. And with that, Tommy raised his arms above his head, stretching out and extending his fingers in an expression of sheer joy. Pink, blue and yellow rainbow glitter shot out from his fingertips. The streams of glitter then streaked out into deep space and on to distant planets. Those planets were then adorned with sparkling halos.

The crowd begins to chant.

WIN WIN WIN! IT'S ALL GOOD! WE GOT THIS! LET'S DO THIS …..

The four contestants appear and the crowd gasps with astonishment. Each of the four contenders are hovering by their assigned corners of the boxing ring: Luchadora Madrugadora (*Queen of Stepford Ken And Barbie Westworld*); Bryanna Dolls (*formerly known as Dyaspora Neosporyn*); Ophelia Wainwright (*Empress of Apathy, Bitoxia, Archaicka, Confederate Region, Isolamicka, Blue Green Planet*) and Clawdeeya Balls (*Doppelgänger of Bryanna Dolls*). They stare each other down cruelly, heartlessly; they impersonate outrageous, ancient Greek heroines dating from Euripides' final creative period of tragic despair. It's clear from the ferocity of their attitudes that they seek to vanquish each other as expediently as possible ……

The semi-finals and then the finals go down over the course of two Blue Green Planet hours. Luchadora Madrugadora makes short work of Bryanna Dolls and Clawdeeya Balls quickly defeats Ophelia Wainwright. For the final contest, Luchadora competes as *The Queen of Maroon-Purple Smoke*; Clawdeeya battles as *The Queen of Gray-Black Smoke*. In the end, due to her persistence, effervescence and superior strength, Luchadora achieves a decisive victory over Clawdeeya Balls. But Clawdeeya is a sore loser who will not accept defeat. Upon confirmation of her losing the match, she howls and screams *UNFAIR! UNFAIR! UNFAIR!* She attacks Tommy Massageny with her Antagonystyck 7000 and then argues with the judges. This goes on for ten agonizingly long minutes. Then, finally realizing that no one cares and that her highly inappropriate temper tantrum will have no effect on the outcome, she vrooms off in a huff, traveling through seven successive wormholes, back to the Via Lactea and the Blue Green Planet. Deep down, she realizes that she's a failure. But she knows that she'll be forgiven by the geopolitically and geographically challenged, celebrity worshipping, brainwashed and even lobotomized inhabitants of BGP. She realizes that as much as she's grotesque, she will be loved, because she's infamous (on BGP *infamous* has just as much value as *famous*). She's so lucky that the morally and ethically compromised BGP population has fallen in love with her abominable persona. They will enable her to maintain her delusions; they will exonerate her for all of her odious traits and worship her as one of their sacred monsters. On BGP, Clawdeeya will be a big fish in a small pond. There, time will heal her wounds and she'll cook up a plan for revenge while she's being idolized by clueless sycophants …..

..... In the meantime, Luchadora laughs and laughs and laughs. It's ludicrous, what Clawdeeya Balls has done and Luchadora is determined to teach Clawdeeya a lesson. Bryanna and Ophelia are both devastated by their respective defeats and neither one of them has ever been a friend of Luchadora. Nonetheless, both of them despise Clawdeeya Balls. So when they approach Luchadora to lay out their plan, in which they'll offer her assistance in challenging their mutual enemy, Luchadora accepts their proposal without hesitation. The three of them then get down to business and start scheming .....

Ophelia and Bryanna: (*speaking simultaneously in the manner of a Greek chorus*) What Clawdeeya Balls has done is reprehensible. She is beyond redemption and we will join with you, Luchadora Madrugadora, to do everything that we can to prevent Clawdeeya's malign power from corrupting and poisoning our beautiful Universe! Such a diabolical representation of femininity does not deserve to exist! She does not love the people of her planet of origin. She has blood on her hands; she committed atrocities on the Blue Green Planet, where she's headed at this very moment! We will find her and once we have captured her, justice will be served .....

Luchadora, Bryanna and Ophelia know that they must pursue Clawdeeya Balls without delay and they whisk themselves away on their silver space chariots. The three women tear through space at the speed of light, to track down Clawdeeya on the Blue Green Planet. They follow the path taken by Clawdeeya through seven successive wormholes. Armed with powerful extraterrestrial incantations, they communicate telepathically as they rocket towards BGP, disguised as their newly assumed identities: Troykana, Tryfectana and Tryumvyrata.

Ophelia and Bryanna: (*speaking simultaneously in the manner of a Greek chorus*) But let's not destroy her right away. Let's have some fun with her! Let's be like cats who play with their prey before killing and consuming it!

Luchadora: Excellent idea, Grrrls! Now listen to the following spell that was inspired by my favorite film, *The Craft*:

I BIND YOU CLAWDEEYA BALLS. YOU AND ALL OF YOUR POWERS WILL BE BOUND, PARALYZED AND IMMOBILIZED. HENCEFORTH YOU WILL BE BOUND FROM CAUSING HARM TO ANY AND ALL LIFE FORMS WITHIN ANY AND ALL OF THE KNOWN MULTIVERSES!

NIHIL OBSTAT! NIHIL OBSTAT! NIHIL OBSTAT!

Ophelia and Bryanna: (*speaking simultaneously in the manner of a Greek chorus*) And let us make her feel the same pain, that all those that she has ever harmed have felt!

DOLOR! NOCERE! DOLOR! NOCERE! DOLOR! NOCERE!

Luchadora: I like your style Grrrls! I think the two of you are on to something!

AGONIA! RETRIBUTIO! AGONIA! RETRIBUTIO! AGONIA! RETRIBUTIO!

Luchadora: Let's put the C back in Charm, Laidies! Three strikes and you're out, Clawdeeya Balls!

Luchadora, Ophelia and Bryanna (*speaking simultaneously in the manner of a Greek chorus*):

We are sad that we -- *Troykana, Tryfectana and Tryumvyrata* -- Will never reach the age of *The Golden Girls*! But it's too late now, there's no time for regrets, the decision has been made! Now it's time for us to transform back into the stardust from which everything that was ever created originates!

FINIS! NIHILUM! FINIS! NIHILUM! FINIS! NIHILUM!

And then with a final burst of warp speed, the trio transmogrify themselves into a fiery asteroid and crash into the Blue Green Planet, causing an explosion with the equivalent force of one billion atomic bombs. By sacrificing themselves, the annihilation of Clawdeeya Balls is assured, along with the unfortunate consequence of terminating all existing life forms on BGP. Miraculously, a group of one hundred survivors, thanks to an advance warning by means of an interstellar telepathic communication, escape BGP before its destruction. As the vessel carrying BGP's refugees is capable of light speed travel, they reach the Androgynous Galaxy in just two weeks, where they colonize a newly discovered world, Renascitur, also known as The Planet of Women. Of the group of one hundred, twenty-five male specimens are brought along to be used for breeding purposes; otherwise, their lives will have little significance. With the establishment of Renascitur, a new era of enlightenment begins .....

PLANET OF WOMEN POEM

And the women were red
And the women had the power
And the men were blue
And they did as they were told
And the men were green
And they were pliant and malleable
Passive, submissive, negligible
Now the shoe was on the other foot
And the women told the men
Walk a kilometer in my shoes
Now you mens got the blues
Women had nothing to lose

GOODBYE FASCIBOOK

Under purple-black clouds, a chilly wind was blowing on an Amourrica Profundan afternoon on the Blue Green Planet. A cross-section of every imaginable human type had congregated, to watch a casket that was about to be lowered into the ground. It was a blue gray coffin, the blue gray being identical to that of the uniforms worn by Amourrica Profundan Post Office employees. A blue gray Thumbs Down logo, against a circular white background, had been ingrained into the center of the cover of the casket. Beneath that logo was an accompanying message, also embedded into the coffin's cover, written in bold white letters in the Vulckana font: IT'S FREE AND IT ALWAYS WILL BE. BUT YOU'LL END UP PAYING A PRICE. BECAUSE ALL OF YOUR REAL LIFE FRIENDSHIPS WILL BE DESTROYED. Who had passed on?

Just as the casket was about to be lowered into the ground, two female mourners forced the proceedings to a halt:

Female Mourner One: Stop! We wanna see who's inside!! We're curious. Could the person in there be the one who stole all of our treasured memories?

Female Mourner Two: Could be, Sister! I'm dying to know what this creep, who allegedly ripped off all of our cherished memories, actually looks like .....

Female Mourner One: I don't care what he, she or IT looks like! All I want is my memories back. Are we actually allowed to take a look inside, to see if this is the one that stole all of our treasured memories?

Female Mourner Two: Well, since we're not related to the corpse, I'm not so sure that would be a good idea. So let's see if anyone else is first. (*raising her voice to speak to the assembled group of mourners*) Does the thing that we think is in this casket have any relatives in attendance? Are there any next-of-kin here who might be able to identify this corpse?

None of the mourners respond.

Female Mourner One: It looks like luck may be on our side today, Grrrlfriend. There are no relatives in attendance; no one who's legally permitted to identify the body.

Female Mourner Two: I'm completely mystified by the reaction of our fellow mourners here. Anyone could identify this corpse, Sister. In fact, at least thirty-three percent of the population of the Blue Green

Planet could identify the body. If the thing that I think is in there, is actually in there, then at least 2.5 billion people would be able to identify this corpse. And FYI BTW ….. IT, that corporation, stole not only the cherished memories of 2.5 billion souls, but also all of the information pertaining to every other aspect of their lives as well!

Female Mourner One: I don't know about you Grrrlfriend, but if this is the thing that I think IT is, who invented the world's most successful, addictive and time-wasting social media site ….. Then I think IT's the equivalent of *Big Brother* and I want me some payback!

Others in the crowd join in.

Male Mourner One: Yeah! You got that right! I could go for some payback too! I'd sure as hell like to get my life back! We wanna see either who, or what, is inside that casket!

The mourners start chanting and clapping.

OPEN UP THE CASKET! OPEN UP THE COFFIN!

The casket is then placed, by four muscular male pallbearers with shaved heads who are dressed in blue gray suits, onto the Monsanto green grass beside the grave. Everyone lines up to have a look inside. The two female mourners open the cover. A casket full of Polaroid Selfishies is revealed.

The mourners start to sing.

DING DONG, FASCIBOOK'S DEAD, FASCIBOOK'S DEAD, FASCIBOOK'S DEAD, DING DONG, FASCIBOOK'S FRACKING DEAD!

Male Mourner One: As if we didn't know what was in there already! And I say what, as opposed to who, because what's in there definitely isn't human!

Male Mourner Two: *So many Selfishies ….. So little time!* Would anyone like to go through all of these Selfishies, to see if there's any good ones? On second thought, they're not worth anything! Everyone knows that Selfishies have no value whatsoever!

Male Mourner One: If there are some good Selfishies in there, then I'd be perfectly willing to like them. But if they're not good, then I'll use that angry face button. I'll have to make do with that, since the dislike button never came into use ….. WHICH I'M MAD AS HELL ABOUT!

Male Mourner Two: Hold on to your horses, my good brother! If Fascibook had ever chosen to put a dislike button into effect, using that button would have torn through the fabric of civilization! You know damn well that the implementation of a dislike button would destroy humanity!

Male Mourner One: To each his own! (*pausing*) Well, now that we know what's inside, how about we proceed with the burial? Because life is short and I'm a busy guy who'd like to get back to wasting time on Twinner again!

Male Mourner Two: Yes, yes, enough already! Close up that casket and get it into the ground. Leave those worthless Selfishies where they are! It was only Fascibook that made us believe that they were valuable! That was Fascibook's special talent. What a quack, a huckster, a charlatan ..... IT learned everything that IT knew from those nineteenth century robber barons! Remember the days when people used to tell you to get a life? Now they'll just tell you to get off Twinner!

The voices of other mourners speak up in agreement with Male Mourner Two. The coffin is then closed and promptly lowered into the ground.

Male Mourner One: Thank the Goddess of Social Media that that's over! Now I can get back on Twinner!

Other mourners start chanting.

LOG ONTO TWINNER, GET BACK ON TWINNER, ZONE OUT ON TWINNER, SPACE OUT ON TWINNER!

Yes, the mourners were happy that Fascibook had left the planet. But now they were stuck with Twinner whether they liked it or not. Twinner was elated; Twinner was watching the entire event via drone. Twinner bore no love for Fascibook; Twinner had been waiting for Fascibook to die. Twinner was ecstatic; Fascibook was gone and now Twinner held the world in the Palm Pilot of its hand ….. No more Freakbook, Geekbook or Greedbook. No more Commiebook, Redstatebook or Bluestatebook. No more Adbook, Algorithmbook, Productbook or Cookthebooks. Fascibook had gone the way of DieSpace.

Female Mourner One: Everyone knows that no social media site is too big to fail, not even a corporate behemoth like Fascibook!

Female Mourner Two: Exactly! Consumers are fickle, they get bored and move on. They'll find a new toy! You'll see, the powers that be will come up with another surefire way to flatten our asses!

Female Mourner One: I know Fascibook treated us poorly. But I'll miss Fascibook; it was a love-hate relationship! It was yin yang, day and night, black and white, dark and light, sun and moon …..

The crowd starts to mourn hysterically. Women are screaming and wailing. Even the men break down into fitful sobs. One man starts laughing continuously while another begins to loudly recite a maniacal monologue about the significance of algorithms.

Male Mourner Three: The Fascibook algorithm sabotaged my Fascibook friendships like a Nazgul-Ringwraith-Death Anorexic!

Male Mourner Four: I'm so incredibly happy that Fascibook has passed on! Now I won't have to sit in Starfucks all day, wasting time on my laptop, being a loser who's pretending to be productive! But beware my friends; Twinner's just as bad! Don't say that I didn't warn you! Oh I know, you think now that Fascibook's gone, you can run into the arms of Twinner to console you! Out of the frying pan ….. Into the fire! Twinner will betray you too, you'll see! Mark my words …..

Female Mourner Three: This isn't the time for a lecture, you cretin! We're grieving; we're in mourning! We're looking for consolation and if that means sloppy seconds with Twinner in our time of need ….. So be it!

Female Mourner Three starts sobbing and screaming, then runs over to a Jaguar XJ sedan, opens the back door, jumps in and slams the door shut. The car lurches forward, the tires scraping over the pebbles of the road as it peels off and away from the proceedings …..

FASCIBOOK EULOGY

The notorious Imogen Havisham, the owner of fif-ty-one percent of the shares of Fascibook, is standing behind a blue gray podium. She is dressed in black, like most of the others in the crowd.

Imogen Havisham: (*haltingly; her speech is punc-tuated by occasional sobs*) Fascibook was my friend, the only friend that I ever had! It sure was great to have a friend who I could log off from whenever I wanted to! That's right; Fascibook and I had an open relationship. Yes, it was complicated! But now Fascibook's left me all alone in this world. Whose wall will I cry on now? Whose posts will I trash and troll when I'm going through bad times and need to deflect my pain onto others? And will I ever be able to block and defriend again? And as for love: do you people think my bank account's going to hold me tight during those long, lonely nights living in my penthouse in Turmerico Tower, Nueva Jork, Puta Jork ..... Without Fascibook? Now that you're gone Fascibook, how will I find meaning in my life? With Fascibook, right from the start I decided to keep things European and let IT go ITS own way when IT wanted to! Because frankly, I wanted my freedom as well. I'm no Betty Draper! I live in the real world ..... That is, when I'm not logged onto Fascibook! And now the only viable alternative seems to be set-tling for a toxic rebound; a *liaison dangereuse* with that two-face Twinner! Everyone knows that Twinner tweens around like nobody's business! (*calmer*) Okay Fascibook, the rumors are true: you were my Frankenstein! You were my Jillary Clintonstein, too! Just one more thing: Let's all be grateful that Fascibook left a child in this world. A child who has become a fully autonomous adult; who'll be there for us *femmes d'un certain age* when the chips are down. That's right, I'm talking about Spinstergram! Who am I kidding? I look in the mirror and see the old Crone from Tarot. While my gentlemen peers are out having a blast, chasing after younger women! But not to worry, I'll have Spinstergram! Spinstergram will soothe me and stroke me with virtual caresses throughout my golden years …..

A female voice interrupts the eulogy to address Imogen Havisham.

Objecting Female Voice: Oh please! You and your sob story! You sure as hell didn't love Fascibook! You owned Fascibook; you controlled Fascibook! You evil capitalist bitch; you tyrannical, plutocratic empress! What the hell do you know about love? You know WHO you loved? You know WHAT you loved? You loved all of your sexual surrogates that you could only afford because of the income that you derived from Fascibook! NEWS FLASH: I loved Fascibook! Did you hear me? I LOVED FASCIBOOK! Fascibook was MY lover! And it wasn't just me. I'm one of many!

There's a whole army of women out there who loved Fascibook! As well as men and an entire gamut of gender fluid types as well; Fascibook was into lots of different kinds of pages! My confession is just the tip of the iceberg! The Pandora's Box will be opening up very soon when a host of disgruntled lovers show up to make claims on your assets! Honey, they'll clean you out and you'll end up living in a trailer ….. Working on the black market and running a meth lab in the Confederate Region ….. If you're lucky!

Voices from the crowd murmur in astonishment.

Objecting Female Voice (*continuing*): So there you have it! I loved Fascibook even though IT could have cared less about fidelity or monogamy! My Grrrlfriends warned me to keep away from players like Fascibook. If only I'd known about all of that illicit liking and sharing that was going on behind my back! Yes IT was mean, cruel, and abusive. IT made Don Draper look like Saint Francis. But IT was better than nothing and Goddess forbid that I be lonely ….. (*hysterically*) You betrayed me Fascibook; you told me that you'd always be there for me! (*out of her mind*) YOU PROMISED ME THAT YOU'D BE BY MY SIDE, HOLDING MY HAND WHEN IT CAME TIME FOR ME TO LOG OFF FROM LIFE! (*calmer*) You know what I want now, Fascibook? I want Deathbook! This whole notion of people being afraid of Deathbook is overrated. With Deathbook, at long last, I'll find peace. I will rest in peace with Deathbook! (*whispering*) I love you, Deathbook ….. (*louder*) I Love You, Deathbook ….. (*shouting*) I LOVE YOU, DEATHBOOK!….. (*shrieking*) I LOVE YOU DEATHBOOK, I'LL LOVE YOU FOREVER AND I LOOK FORWARD TO OUR LIFE TOGETHER IN ETERNITY!

The Objecting Female Voice starts to chant.

DEATHBOOK! DEATHBOOK! DEATHBOOK! DEATHBOOK!

Gradually everyone in attendance joins in, chanting *DEATHBOOK* while clapping and dancing to the cacophony. Some of the mourners bang on pots and pans. Others play various instruments of percussion: castanets, maracas, triangles, tambourines and washboards. Still others of the bereaved jam on accordions, harmonicas and kazoos. A clown, in clown white makeup, is wearing a baggy red and white striped suit with a bright blue tie and a yellow dress shirt. He's also sporting a red fright wig, red nose, red lips, red and yellow gloves, and red and yellow floppy clown shoes. He's playing a tuba. A crazy hippie laidie wearing a yellow, green, pink and purple Grateful Dead-style tie-dyed dress plays the recorder and dances merrily. Others soon join in to trip the light fantastic ….. Hari Krishnas, Goths, break-dancers, skateboarders, steampunks, Moonies, Trekkies, Scientologists, Burning Man and Renaissance Fair participants appear out of nowhere to shake their

Fascibook groove things. The mourners forget about their despair and are now feeling cheerful .....

All of a sudden, the Crazy Hippie Laidie stops playing her recorder and addresses the crowd.

Crazy Hippie Laidie: Hear me everyone! HEAR ME ..... Listen well, brothers and sisters: You've got it all wrong! Sweet Violet Seventh Chakra Goddess: Deathbook is not the answer! The answer is, was and always will be: Lifebook! So no more Deathbook! Deathbook be gone! Here's to life! Here's to LIFEBOOK!

The Crazy Hippie Laidie starts chanting and clapping and the crowd follows her lead.

LIFEBOOK! LIFEBOOK! LIFEBOOK! LIFEBOOK!

Meanwhile back in *them thar piney woods* ..... Big Mama and her son Bobby stand in the open doorway of their trailer, looking up at the carpet of brilliant stars above them. Their pupils, irises and the whites of their eyes remain pitch black. They're smiling with satisfaction due to the good works that they've achieved. They're beaming with pride over the contributions that they've made to humanity. Because they are The People.

AUTHOR SELF-PORTRAIT

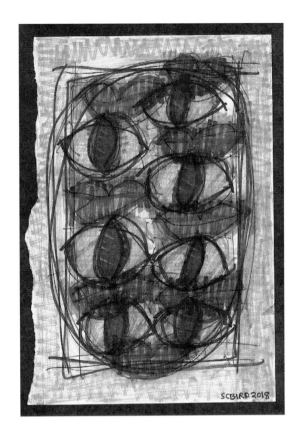

"New Headshots"
Stephen C. Bird, 2018

ABOUT THE AUTHOR

Stephen C. Bird is a fiction writer and visual artist. His books include "Hideous Exuberance" (2009, 2013); "Catastrophically Consequential" (2012); and "Any Resemblance To A Coincidence Is Accidental" (2015). Mr. Bird was born in Toronto, Ontario and grew up in Erie County, New York. He lived in New York City for thirty-three years and currently resides in Canada.

"Ongoing Confusion"
Stephen C. Bird, 2017

"Six Faces"
Stephen C. Bird, 2017

"Six Faces Further"
Stephen C. Bird, 2018

"Four Faces"
Stephen C. Bird, 2016

'Three Two Faces"
Stephen C. Bird, 2014

"Seven Frazzled Faces"
Stephen C. Bird, 2018

"Change Of Scene"
Stephen C. Bird, 2018